Books by Jess W

Sparkling

Sparkling Stilettos
Sparkling Stars

Sparkling

SPARKLING STARS

JESS WRIGHT

Dedication

This is dedicated to the most important people in my life who inspire me every day to live my dreams.

My mum. You're my best friend, my hero and the kindest person I know. Thank you for being a 'pushy mum' and making me do everything possible to enable me to reach my dreams. This book reflects me in every way, my dreams that have always been larger than life, the glitter, the drama, the glam, the ambition, the romanticism, and most importantly the want to see the world and not settle for anything less. It's you, Mum, who instilled that in me and helped me achieve what I have today. Thank you for putting me into an amazing school even if we could not afford it, thank you for taking me to dancing, singing and acting five times a week and making me a packed lunch! Thank you for telling me to quit my job and follow my dreams and never give up.

My dad. A man whose smile lights up the room and who has the kindest eyes and heart ever. Your strength and hard work is what has made us kids who we are. Without your support we would never have had half the chance of achieving our dreams. I am similar to you in so many ways and for that I couldn't be prouder. Thank you for showing me that in life it really is nice to be nice.

My siblings. Mark, Joshua and Natalya. You all make me prouder every day. Your ambition, determination and kind heartedness are just a few attributes that make you all the best brothers and sister I could have.

My grandparents. The pillar to our family's strength and the light in all our lives. I'm so grateful to have such amazing grandparents who have been there for me every step of the way. Nanny Irene, the most dignified, regal and intelligent lady I know. Nanny Pat, the kindest, funniest and most sincere angel to grace our lives. Grandad Eddie, the stem to this family's graciousness and heart. You are the most wonderful man I know, thank you for making the impossible seem possible. PS: You know it makes sense. Grandad Charlie, now an angel in heaven. You have been so missed since passing but in our thoughts every day. The loving, sensitive, charismatic man that was the life and soul of every party and we all miss dearly.

To my beautiful cousins, too many to mention I love you all. Cousins by blood, best friends by choice.

To my bestest girlfriends, Kelly, Gabby, Sade, Lucy, Krystee and Lauren. I have spent the majority of my thirty years sharing the most hilarious times of my life with you girls. I know we will be in each other's lives until the end. Here's to the next thirty years! So glad I found you all.

Krystal and Hannah, thank you for putting up with me and making me feel like a goddess even on my worst days! True friends forever. Benji, you fill me with joy as well as pick up all my pieces day by day. Thank you.

Courtney, Charlotte and Lauren, thank you for being at most of my appearances and putting a smile on my face so often. PS. Stop buying me chocolate!

Finally thank you to everyone who has supported me through everything and especially bought this book.

I love you all.

1

Excuse me, excuse me, coming through, emergency, emergency."

Megan turned at the sound of a familiar voice.

"Sorry, so sorry." Brendon, tall, ginger and wearing a cerise T-shirt with 'Rainbow Lover' stamped across the front, was barging past several scowling passengers waiting to purchase tickets. "Can't be helped, though, crisis situation." He tilted his chin in the air, tugged at his roll-along case and set his attention on Megan.

"What the...?" Megan said, glancing back at the British Airways employee she'd just been speaking to.

"There you are," Brendon said. "Seriously, you are a hard woman to track down in a place as big as this." He bumped into the ticket desk and banged his passport on top of it.

"What are you doing here?" Megan asked.

"What do you think?" He rolled his eyes. His cheeks were flushed and several strands of hair were stuck to his forehead. Megan knew he would be complaining about that in a minute, and teasing it back to its usual carefully flicked style.

"I have no idea..." Megan said, though she couldn't deny that she wasn't thrilled to see one of her best friends in the world at her side. Especially when things had gone so wrong and she'd been so desperate that running away had been her only option.

Brendon turned to the airline lady. "I'll have what she's having."

"What...?" Megan said. "What do you mean?"

"Where is she going?" Brendon asked, indicating the ticket that had just been set over the top of Megan's passport.

"She's going to Los Angeles, lucky thing." The heavily

made-up woman gave a big grin.

Brendon let out a whistle. "Wow, I'll have me some of that." He slapped a credit card down over his passport. "Are we travelling first class, sweetpea?"

"Er, no, not this time." Megan had never travelled first class. But she would one day. She'd make sure of it. She had big plans for the future, just as soon as she got over this hiccup.

"I guess you want to sit together?"

"Yes, please." Brendon nodded and wiped his fingers over his brow. "We have *lots* to talk about."

"Are you sure about this?" Megan asked. "I'm on a one-way ticket. I don't know where I'm staying or when I'll be back."

"Oh, yes, of course I'm sure." He rubbed his hands together and grinned. "It sounds like the best type of adventure, and somewhere so glamorous too. Just think, this time tomorrow we'll be strolling down Rodeo Drive. I've got a friend working there by the way—we can go to the Dolby Theatre and see the stars, drink champers in the Beverley Wilshire and pretend to be Julia Roberts and Richard Gere. Oh, just think of all the hot men there'll be. I vote we head straight down to Muscle Beach. We'll sit and drink cocktails and watch the...waves!" He winked and licked his lips. "The waves of muscle and rippling abs, that is."

His enthusiasm was infectious and Megan giggled, a bubble of excitement rushing through her for the first time. Up until this point it had been all about getting away, removing herself from London and Dylan and the nightmare that had become her and James. But now, with Brendon at her side, it all seemed much more fun.

"What made you decide on LA?" Brendon asked. "Not that I'm complaining."

"Luck of the draw," the airline lady said, handing Brendon the machine to key in his PIN. "She just asked for a ticket on the next plane out of here. Very romantic and exciting."

"You didn't just say that?" Brendon paused and gawped at Megan. "What if you'd ended up in Syria or Senegal or Siberia?"

"Would you have still come with me?" Megan raised her eyebrows.

Brendon hesitated. "Yes, of course." He keyed in his number. "I'd travel anywhere with you, you know that. You need me."

"Well I won't deny I'm not over the moon to see you." She thought for a moment. "But what about Gucci? Where is he? He needs you too." Megan had rarely seen Brendon parted from Gucci, his adorable Pomeranian.

"He's at my mother's. I swung by and dropped him off on my way to the airport."

"But you'll miss him terribly. And he'll pine for you." Megan was worried. She adored Gucci—he'd been a little hero the night before when she'd needed all the heroes she could get.

"Of course I will, but he'll be fine. He loves Mum's choice of fluffy conservatory cushions. He'll spend all day and all night humping them. If he can't get to your cat doorstop, they're his second choice."

🐾 🐾 🐾

Two hours later, Megan and Brendon were settling themselves into row twenty-six, seats A and B. Brendon took the window, and Megan was happy in the middle. Sitting on a plane, about to be whisked over the Atlantic to a different country, far, far away was exactly what she needed.

"I can't believe you cancelled that last appearance on *Ralph and Jayne*?" Brendon said, clipping his seatbelt. "That was quite a coup to get that for you."

Megan sighed. "I know. I feel bad, really I do, for throwing it away like that. But I'd done two appearances and I'm sure Enid will handle it perfectly when she calls to explain

I can't do the last one. Knowing her, she'll keep it open so I can do another when I get back. She's very professional."

"Who is this Enid?"

"Oh, you haven't met her, have you? She's my new assistant. Georgie sorted her out for me. She's great."

"Well Georgie wouldn't send you a dud, would she?" He tutted.

"Of course not, she's great at her job. But Enid really is special, she's only just started but has got a great handle already on Winter Shoes and how I operate. She's super-organised and super-efficient." She was also quite motherly, which appealed to Megan as her mother lived in Sydney now, but she kept that to herself. She tried to be brave when it came to missing her family, who'd emigrated a few years ago.

"Well this Enid must have impressed you if you've left your business, and by that I mean your baby, in her hands."

"She has." Megan paused. "But I haven't left her completely alone, I'll be at the end of the phone or on email. I can run it remotely, do as much as necessary."

"Don't forget about the time difference."

"I won't. But to tell you the truth, I was going to take some downtime anyway. I've got a pile of designs rattling around my head I want to work on. A whole season and a collection of bridal shoes that I need to get from my imagination onto paper and then made up as prototypes. And I just can't seem to concentrate with so much other stuff going on."

"Like what?"

"You know, office stuff. When I'm there and I start on something the phone goes or an email comes in that needs urgent attention. I need peace to design, peace and quiet and hours of *me* time."

Brendon pressed his hand over his heart. "You're such a true artist, a tortured soul struggling to release the genius inside."

"Don't be silly." Megan grinned. "I just get distracted

by the day job. It's not been easy being the designer, the secretary, the general dogsbody *and* the CEO of a business."

"Well at least you haven't had to worry about hiring staff, Georgie's done that for you, or PR and marketing, because you have *moi*." He swirled his hand in the air then pointed at himself.

"And I couldn't do it without you, either of you." She squeezed his arm. "I really do appreciate all you do for Winter Shoes, Brendon."

"I know you do. Though I might have to start charging for my services soon." He laughed. "Mates' rates, naturally."

"Of course I'll pay you, and not mates' rates, full rates." She shook her head. "I should have already, we'll get something sorted out. I promise."

"Hey, hey don't worry about it. I'm all good, Winter Shoes is something I'm passionate about too and I like seeing you happy. I've got enough ticking along with my other freelance work." He paused. "But let's see what happens in LA."

"Do you mean in general or for Winter Shoes?"

The engines suddenly roared to life and Megan was pressed back in her seat.

"Oh sweet Lord." Brendon gripped the armrest. "I always hate this bit."

"It's okay," Megan reassured him. They were hurtling down the runway, the plane bumping as the speed grew.

The front of the plane lifted smoothly into the air. Megan felt her stomach float and she looked out of the window at the ground shrinking into the distance.

"There we go, we're up," she said.

Brendon nodded, still staring straight ahead.

"We'll get you a drink in a minute." Megan rested her hand over his.

"Yes, yes, that will be good." His voice was a little high.

Once the plane had levelled and the seatbelt sign had gone off, the airhostess came along with the drinks trolley. They each ordered a white wine and Brendon added Pringles to his request.

"Cheers," he said, touching the rim of his glass to Megan's. "Here's to LA."

"And adventures." Megan took a sip of her wine. "So what did you mean about what happens in LA? Did you mean for Winter Shoes? You said you know someone who works on Rodeo Drive? You've never told me that before."

"Well you know what it's like, he's a friend of a friend. He works at LA Hype, a cute fashion boutique that sells everything from shoes to handbags, jewellery to midi-dresses. I've seen it online, looks adorable and in an amazing location, right between Prada and Agent Provocateur with those cute little lollipop trees in tubs out front. We simply must go and hang out there. Maybe we can afford a pair of socks." He laughed.

"Sounds great."

"It will be. He's pretty damn cute too."

"Who is?"

"This friend of a friend." He tutted. "Zane, his name is, used to live in Chelsea but headed out to LA a few years ago with a boyfriend, now ex-boyfriend from what I gather, to work in the fashion industry. Got a degree from some London uni and then hitched his wagon to the stars and now mingles with the famous and the Beverley Hills clan."

"Good for him." Megan nodded. That was what she wanted to do, hitch her wagon to the stars and hang on for the ride. She had no intention of letting go until she reached dizzying heights and mingled with top designers and people who made a difference in the fashion world. It was the way she was wired, ambition ran hot in her veins. And now, with no Dylan to hold her back, she could throw all her time and efforts into Winter Shoes — once this little blip was over, of course.

"So what really happened?" Brendon asked. "To make you want to jump on the first flight out of the country to anywhere."

"Well last night was bad enough, wasn't it?" Megan said,

supressing a shudder at the memory of her ex-fiancé — whom she'd jilted at the altar — turning up at her flat deluded about what was still between them and determined to win her back. He'd scared her with his adamant belief that he could win her round when she'd been crystal clear about the fact they were over. She couldn't have been any blunter with words or actions — after all, she had turned and run, run as fast as she could in sparkly stilettoes down the aisle and away from him. She'd craved freedom, fresh air, to be her own person again, not controlled by him from the moment she woke up until she went to sleep at night.

But dumping someone who was as domineering as Dylan wasn't a walk in the park, in fact, it was more like being an extra on *Nightmare on Elm Street*. He'd raged and cried and tried to win her round with kisses she hadn't wanted. He'd even bought her a new ring, so they could start afresh, and dropped to one knee begging her to go back.

As if!

"Megan?" Brendon asked, tipping his head as though encouraging her to go on.

"He put another note under my door," Megan said. "Last night."

"What? After I left?" Brendon banged his fist into his palm. "He must have been lurking about out there, in the shadows. Oh, if only I'd seen him."

"Yes, he does that — lurk in the shadows — but I'm glad you didn't see him and approach him. He's unpredictable."

"Unpredictable and a creep. No, wait, I mean stalker."

"That is what it's felt like."

"I'm sure." He pulled a sympathetic face. "What did the note say?"

"Basically it said I was his and he would get me back, soon. Really short and precise, like he was *telling* me, not *asking* me to get back with him."

"He's got a nerve."

"Well yes, he's always had that. But it was like…"

"What?"

13

"Like he was going to kidnap me or something." She stared out of the window at the huge marshmallow clouds billowing into the distance. This had been the best thing for her, to be heading out of London, out of the UK and with no one knowing where she was. No, make that the only thing for her to do.

"Well this is the best thing for you," Brendon said, starting on his Pringles. "You couldn't stay, sweetpea, you just couldn't."

"I know. But there's more."

"More?"

"Yes, he was at my office this morning. First thing."

"Oh hang me from the rafters and call me batty, you cannot be serious?" His eyes widened and he shoved several crisps into his mouth. He began to munch, clearly enjoying the drama.

"Unfortunately I am being serious, he was just skulking around out there. He wanted me to let him in."

"Please tell me you'd locked the door, you're terrible for forgetting to do that." A flash of panic crossed his face.

"Not anymore I'm not, and I don't think I ever will be again, not after turning around in my kitchen last night and finding Dylan there, having just strutted into the place like he owned it."

"Well, thank heavens for that locked office door. What did he want?"

"Same as before, for me to go back to him. Marry him, have his babies, blah, blah, blah, whatever…" She twirled her finger next to her ear. "Cuckoo. Completely stark raving mad."

"He really launches not being able to take a hint up to a whole new level that's for sure."

Megan huffed and drank some of her wine. "He was just going on and on, talking on his phone but standing on the other side of the window. Saying how he couldn't live without me and we could make it work." She paused. "He also confessed to being the one to have made all the silent phone calls."

"Well, you don't have to be Einstein to work that out." Brendon shoved in more crisps. After he'd eaten he said, "So how did you get rid of him? Police?"

"No, but to tell you the truth I wasn't far off calling them. It gave me the shivers, it was so early, no one else was about, not even the estate agents next door, and let's face it, a pane of glass isn't much of a barrier."

Brendon looked aghast. "You really think he would have smashed it?"

"I honestly don't know what he's capable of anymore. I thought I knew him so well for all those years. Thought I loved him too, but now, lately, his behaviour has made him like a different person to me. I always knew I'd hurt him by ending it, and I admit I could have made it less dramatic, but he's obsessed with getting what he wants."

"Yes I agree, but, Megan, it was glorious to see you holding up your dress and running down the aisle like that. A perfect scene from *Runaway Bride*, hair flowing, chest heaving, veil floating behind you like a ghostly trail of smoke."

"I didn't wear a veil."

"Well, my imagination embellishes these glorious moments."

"Brendon. It really wasn't meant to be glorious."

"I say it how I see it, or remember it. Excuse me..." He held up his hand to a passing airhostess who was pushing the drinks trolley. "Two more wines, please."

"Certainly, sir." She handed two small bottles over the elderly man sitting to Megan's right. He had his earphones in and his eye mask on. Megan hoped he'd stay that way.

"Thanks, lovely," Brendon said to the airhostess then set both tiny bottles down on Megan's tray.

"I don't want two."

"I know you don't, one is for me." He fiddled with his table tray for a moment then once it was flat again, took a bottle and poured the wine into his own glass.

"We mustn't get drunk," Megan said with a giggle. She was already a little woozy after just one drink.

"Why not? We're on holiday now." Brendon grinned.

"Mmm, yes, I suppose that's how we should look at it."

"Absolutely. I know you want to work on designs but let's have a few days of fun as we adjust to the time zone."

"Sounds like a plan." Her heart was feeling lighter with each passing mile the jet engines took her towards America. Getting away from Dylan and James was a good thing.

An image of James hovered in her mind. Well, maybe getting away from James wasn't such a good thing. They'd had something special going on, really special, hot, sexy special. He was everything she looked for in a guy yet she'd gone and ruined it. Well, she hadn't, Dylan had.

"So now what's going through that pretty head of yours?" Brendon asked, studying her. "No." He held up his glass. "Don't tell me. Hot Guy."

"James, you mean."

"Yes, that's the one, Hot Guy James."

Megan shrugged. She'd called James Carter Hot Guy too, until they'd been properly introduced. She hadn't got as far as introducing him to her friends — their fledgling relationship, although intense, hadn't moved that far forward. "He's not an easy person to forget."

"He didn't get back to you then?"

"No, I even sent him a text. He read it, you can tell on iPhones can't you, but nothing. Not even a call for me to explain and he never answered when I tried to call him."

"I have to say that's all a bit off." Brendon frowned. "Like really off."

"I guess what he saw through the kitchen window was pretty damning. He wasn't to know that while Dylan was holding me close and attempting to kiss me I was trying to untangle myself and push him away. Things aren't always what they seem but people do tend to jump to conclusions."

"He could have given you a chance to explain that it was your idiot ex, though." Brendon rolled his eyes and tutted.

"Maybe I'd used my chances up with him." Megan shook her head, remembering how she'd left him in the rain outside her office after their first kiss, then how she'd panicked after spending the night at his house and slipped away in the morning while he was showering and making breakfast. She'd apologised for both of course, but perhaps a third strike had been the final nail in the coffin of their relationship. Some things were just not meant to be, even when it felt like they should be.

"It's his loss," Brendon said. "Because you are without doubt the best thing that's ever happened to him."

"Well I don't know about that—"

"I don't care how many awards he's got, or how amazing a director he is, if he hasn't got a good woman at his side, and by that I mean you, then he's a loser."

"But—"

Brendon held up his hands. "I know what you're going to say, that he's made a difference with all the documentaries he's made. That he's brave and loyal and passionate about justice, but still...he's a moron." He paused for breath. "Exposing malfunctioning weapons used by the British military might get him as many accolades as threats, but it's still not won me over."

"Blimey, did you memorise his Wikipedia page?"

"No... Well I read it a couple of times, and why not, it's got some nice pictures of him and he's pretty easy on the eye."

He most certainly was. Tall and lean with an athletic rather than a gym-honed body, James held himself with style and ease. He was comfortable in his own skin. His often brooding face gave away the seriousness with which he took his job and the world he lived in, but once relaxing and smiling he became an easy companion with a quick smile and keen wit.

"Shame he's not—" Brendon started.

"He's most definitely not gay."

"Doesn't even swing both ways?" Brendon looked

hopeful.

"I would say not." Megan thought back to their one night together and how he'd held her, kissed her, made her feel so special, like the only woman in the world. For that night she *had* been the only woman in his world. She'd hoped for more, but a combination of factors had dashed that hope like petals being ripped from a rose in a hurricane.

She sighed. No point in thinking about what could have been. That was in the past now. Time to think of the future, both long-term and immediate.

"So where are we going to stay when we get there?" Brendon asked as if guessing her next thought.

"A hotel I guess, but I'm not sure where. I've never been to LA before."

"I reckon it's one of those places that will feel familiar, though."

"What do you mean?"

"Because it's on TV so much. A bit like New York."

"Mmm, so what do you think? Beverley Hills?"

"I think that might break the bank, darling. I say let's head to the beach, must be somewhere in Santa Monica with rooms."

Megan laughed. "I know exactly what you're up to."

"I'm not up to anything." He hung his mouth open as if shocked.

Megan poked him in the ribs, still giggling. "You just want to be as near as possible to all those buff, oiled bodies as you can. I can see I'm going to have problems with you in LA, Brendon Trugate."

"How very dare you." There was a twinkle in his eye. "I'll be on my absolute best behaviour. Scout's honour." He held three fingers to his chest, pinkie and thumb touching.

"Mmm, I'll believe that when I see it, but I'm guessing you are thanking your lucky stars that ticket wasn't for Siberia."

"I don't know, there's something about a big, hairy Russian that's quite appealing."

2

"Hey, Georgie, how are you?"

"Megan, oh thank goodness. I've been worried sick."

"Hang on, I'll put you on speaker, Brendon is here."

"Brendon is there! What the...?" Georgie's voice went a pitch higher.

Megan fiddled with her phone.

"Hey, Pudding and Pie," Brendon said, pushing his sunglasses up onto the top of his head. "How is the most loved-up girl in the world today?"

"Well I'd be better if I wasn't wondering what the hell is going on. Where are you, for heaven's sake?"

"Well..." Megan said, glancing out to sea.

From the balcony of their hotel room they could see the huge waves of the Pacific rolling towards the shore. They were topped with surfers who flicked this way and that riding the crests. "Let's just say we have a rather nice view."

"Of what?"

"Sun, sea and surfers," Brendon said, nodding approvingly and rubbing his hands together.

"Stop teasing," Georgie whined. "Where are you? I'm guessing it's not Bognor?"

Megan giggled. "Hardly, we're currently in our very expensive hotel room in Santa Monica. The balcony overlooks the beach and has views of the pier and Ferris wheel."

"It's to die for," Brendon said. "I'll send you some pics." He reached for his iPhone.

"You jammy buggers," Georgie said. "Wish I was in LA. I've always want to go there."

"No, you don't wish you were here," Megan said. "You'd miss Tom too much." Megan knew Georgie would pine terribly for her new fiancé if an ocean and continent separated them.

"Well, yes...but..."

"There's no reason why you can't join us," Brendon said, clicking away as a particularly handsome and topless skateboarder whizzed by on the path below, his dark hair in a bun and his skin the colour of a perfect apple-pie crust. He had a swirling tattoo that covered half his arm and his abs were bricked.

"Knock me down with a feather duster, I'm in heaven," Brendon murmured.

"What was that?" Georgie asked.

"I'll send it to you because no words can describe." He sighed. "You'll know why I'm in heaven then." Brendon tapped the screen and sent the image to Georgie.

"How come you're in LA, though? What happened?" Georgie asked.

"It was all too much, with Dylan and everything. I had to get away, my feet itched to get away. I just couldn't stay in London another day and with Enid in the office, thanks to you, I decided to just go with my instincts."

"Well I'm glad you have so much confidence in Enid — Oh, wow..."

"See?" Brendon said, shielding his eyes from the sun and peering into the distance as the boarder disappeared.

"Blimey, yes I should think you are in heaven," Georgie said then whistled. "He's gorgeous."

"And it's what they all look like, seriously." Brendon spun on his chair, searching for his next person to admire.

"Well keep the pictures coming." Georgie laughed.

"We will, and I am sorry you're not here. Are you okay?" Megan asked.

"Yes, fine. That little spat about the stag night is all sorted, and Tom has even taken it upon himself to book a couple of venues for us to go and check out this weekend for the reception. And then Mum and I are going to look at dresses on my day off."

"That's exciting." A pang of regret hit Megan. She'd always imagined she'd go with her best friend to choose her wedding dress. The way Georgie had when she'd picked the one she'd walked down the aisle in to marry Dylan. Well, not-marry Dylan as it had turned out.

"Yes, it is, we'll set a date soon. The minute we have the venues tied down."

"Can't wait," Megan said.

"So excited for another wedding," Brendon added.

"Have you got Gucci there?" Georgie asked.

"No, he's with my mother, she'll be spoiling him rotten with fillet steak and steamed chicken. He'll be like a beach ball when I get home, more pork pie than Pomeranian."

"Why didn't you take him? You can these days."

"Not enough time to organise that," Brendon said. "It was all a bit last minute."

"We could have him flown out," Megan said.

"Mmm. That's an idea." Brendon tapped the side of his head.

"Whoa, how long are you intending to stay? Is this more than a holiday? More than an escape for a few days?"

"We don't know yet?" Megan looked at Brendon.

He shrugged. "We'll see what comes along."

"What do you mean?"

"There might be some opportunities for Winter Shoes. I have contacts here, you know."

"Rodeo Drive contacts," Megan said.

"Wow, exciting stuff, but…"

"What?" Brendon asked.

"Ring me lots, send photos, keep me in the loop."

"We will," Megan said. "And you do the same. We want all the details on the venues and the dress, and when we get back we'll help with the other stuff. Oh, and I'll get some designs down for your bridal shoes too. I'll be inspired by the sun sand and surf."

"Hey, I don't want flip-flops." Georgie laughed.

"You'll get the most amazing sparkling stilettoes ever

made."

"I know I will."

"Come on, chop chop," Brendon said. "Enough chatter, we have things to see, places to go, people to do. We'll catch you later, Georgie, and send you our tourist pics of the Hollywood sign and Muscle Beach."

Georgie laughed again. "Yes, I know which pics I'm likely to get the most of."

"There'll be cultural ones too," Megan said. "Speak to you soon. Take care."

"Yep, you too."

Megan ended the call and turned to Brendon. He was leaning over the balcony staring out to sea.

"You okay?" she asked.

"Yes, totally. I needed this too, you know. An escape, a break, it's all been getting me down a bit."

"What has?"

"One-night stands. It's all good fun but it would be nice to have a man who truly cared about me, wanted to spend time with me, get to know what's in here" — he tapped his chest—"rather than just a roll in the sack."

Megan put her hand on his shoulder. "The right man is waiting for you. I can feel it in my bones."

"You think?" He turned to her, his face unusually serious.

"Yes, of course. And he may even be here, in this city where dreams come true."

He smiled, a lovely wide smile that went right to his eyes. "Yep, you're right, so what are we waiting for. Come on, let's go explore."

Megan blew out a breath. Her cheeks were hot and her brow damp. Her pale pink vest top was sticking to her back. "Blimey, it's hot up here."

"It is, but worth it, look." Brendon pointed ahead.

They'd hiked high along a trail in Griffith Park and now stood directly behind the Hollywood sign.

"It's pretty impressive," Megan said, slotting her shades on the top of her head.

"Freaking awesome," Brendon added inflecting an American twang on the last word.

"You can see so far." Megan studied the sprawl of homes and skyscrapers before her. A dusty smog hugged the horizon to the east but to the west, where the ocean faded into the distance, the air was clear and uninterrupted by even a single cloud.

Brendon took a photograph in each direction. "I'll whizz these to Georgie."

"Good idea, though it will be middle of the night in the UK."

"She'll get them in the morning. She'll know we were thinking of her."

"Yes." Megan was quiet for a moment, enjoying the view and standing still. "You know, maybe you should bring Gucci over. He could fly on his own, in the hold, couldn't he?"

"I don't know. What if we only stay a week?"

"We won't, will we." Megan gestured before them. "We've so much to explore and he'd love it here."

"He would, you're right, he's a sucker for style and sophistication and being in the right place at the right time."

Megan giggled. "Yes, he is." She felt light and free. A million miles from her problems with Dylan. Even the ache in her chest that appeared every time she thought of James wasn't as intense now she had a plan, something to do.

She studied the tallest building in the cluster of towering blocks. She wondered what James was doing. Was he heading off to make another dangerous documentary? Perhaps he was taking some downtime now that *Poor Choices* was complete. Maybe he was sunning himself around a pool in Spain, or catching rays in the Maldives. Wherever he was, she was sure it wouldn't take him long to move on in the romance department.

There it was. The pain she'd thought had lessened. It was

still there in all its spiteful glory.

The possibility of James with someone else stung like a thousand bees. It twisted her heart and made her guts tense. She just didn't want that image in her head. His lips had been hers to kiss, his smiles hers to enjoy, and his touch, his caresses…they'd stroked her soul and made her feel alive again. Like a woman who was falling in love and being romanced. Megan didn't want anyone else but her to have James' affection.

She turned from the view and looked down at the dusty ground. She had no right to feel such possession, she knew she didn't, but it was the way her heart beat.

"You okay?" Brendon asked.

"Yeah, just hot."

"Sure?"

She didn't think Brendon didn't want to hash through it all again with her. She'd messed up with Hot Guy and that was the end of story. "Absolutely." She smiled. "Come on, where next?"

"Where next? There's only one place next for us, sweetpea, and that's Rodeo Drive. You're going to be in shoe paradise."

Megan rubbed her hands together. "Well what are we waiting for?"

They made their way back along the trail and caught a bus that took them down the winding road. Megan shut her eyes on some of the hairpin bends, not wanting to look at the steep drops that would take them to their grave should there be some mishap with the wheels.

After stopping for a cool lemonade and a freshen-up, they stepped onto the famous Rodeo Drive.

"Blimey O'Riley," Brendon said, linking arms with Megan. "I can't believe that I'm finally here, standing on this very street. I've had wet dreams about this."

"It looks so…expensive," Megan said, admiring the pristine canopies that hooded many of the shop windows. Some were plain, others striped, and a few had patterns on them. Most shops had neat topiary plants out the front and some had even gone as far as having strips of red carpet. Every few feet, wrought-iron posts held hanging baskets dripping with flowers.

"That's because it *is* expensive, super expensive. Come on, even if we can't afford anything we can still look."

"And be inspired."

"Exactly."

A woman with an enormous red hat, dark shades and two giant black poodles tottered past them. The dogs were on red leads and held their chins up haughtily, the same way their owner did.

Megan twisted her head to watch them walk past.

Brendon did the same. "That's it," he said, "I've decided. I'll ask Mother dearest to put Gucci on the next flight out, he's all good to go. He'd be blissed out on Rodeo Drive, it's simply too cruel not to allow him this experience."

Megan squeezed his arm. "Great, I can't wait for him to get here."

Brendon grinned. "Right, now to go and meet Zane, if he still works there, that is." He rubbed his teeth with his finger and patted his hair, which was perfectly neat and coiffed.

"You look beyond handsome, as always," Megan said.

"Good, because Zane is a hottie, and with an LA tan, I should think he's even hotter."

They made their way past the palm trees that lined the pavement and a café with elegant customers positioned beneath parasols being served by a waitress who looked like a supermodel. Sleek cars, mainly black, rolled quietly by. A bright yellow Lamborghini disturbed the peace with a thumpy beat, the handsome silver-fox occupier bobbing his head to the tune and looking as cool as a slab of ice.

Megan suppressed a shiver of excitement that trickled down her spine. Like Brendon, she'd always wanted to visit Rodeo Drive. But not for the shopping, no, she wanted to be on the other side, she wanted her goods, her shoes, to be on display here. So that the rich, beautiful folk who wiled away their hours flexing their plastic could snap up her designs and show them off to their friends.

Prada came into view. Elegant yet majestic. The windows were adorned with tall, skinny mannequins draped in the latest fashions. A security guy who looked like he'd stepped out of *Men in Black* stood on a black carpet with PRADA stamped in gold on it. His arms were crossed and he stared straight ahead.

"Maybe I should cause a scene just so I can have him grab me," Brendon mumbled.

Megan looked away and giggled. "I wouldn't put it past you."

"Maybe later, look, here's LA Hype."

They stopped outside a smaller boutique that had one enormous window set in what looked like a mahogany frame. The front door was as tall as the window, and made of reflective glass—it had LAH engraved on it. In the window was a single mannequin on a *Wizard of Oz* style bicycle complete with basket on the front. Her hair stuck out behind her as though the wind had caught it. She wore a tight flowery dress, had flowers in her hair and wore the most ridiculous heels ever for riding a bike. But they were nice heels, satin covered and embroidered with small pink flowers to match the dress.

"Don't be fooled by the hippy look," Brendon said. "Ain't nothing in here a hippy could afford."

"So, shall we go in? Meet this Zane guy? Check it out?"

"He might not be at work today, if he's still an employee that is."

"Well we won't know if we stand out here, will we?" Megan tugged his arm. "Come on."

"Okay." Brendon took a deep breath.

Megan pushed the door and stepped inside. The scent of the hanging baskets outside and the heated pavement was replaced with a sweet powdery smell that held a hint of grapefruit. The warmth of the sun switched to a cool cloak of air conditioning that settled over her shoulders.

The door shut behind them and Megan looked around.

It was the most perfect shop she'd ever seen. Not too big, not too small. The floor was made of the same wood that clad the outside and was rich and polished. The walls held racks and rails containing clothes, only one of each item, and shoes of all shapes and sizes but each design exquisite. Silk drapes in the palest peach led the way to changing rooms and the till was set discreetly next to a bunch of flowers so big Megan wondered how they'd got them through the door.

"You like?" Brendon asked, glancing around.

"Yes, very much so." She stepped up to a round table in the centre of the shop that was draped with garlands of fresh flowers and held an assortment of shoes displayed on baskets, like the one on the bike.

"Look at this," she said, holding up a moss-green stiletto that had embroidered ivy wending up the heel and fanning out over the back of the shoe. "It's luscious."

"Can I help you?"

Megan and Brendon turned at the sound of a deep voice behind them. Megan still held the shoe.

"We are just, er, looking," Megan said.

The man standing before her was tall and slim, had a light tan and his blond hair was parted on the side and coiffed the way Brendon did his. He wore a flowery shirt that was done up to the collar and he had unbelievably tight pale green jeans on.

"Zane?" Brendon said, placing his hand on his hip.

The man peered more closely at Brendon. "Well I never," he said, his face cracking into a broad smile. "You're Callum's mate, aren't you?"

"Yes, Brendon Trugate. How are you doing?"

"Great, yeah, great." He wafted his hand in Brendon's direction. "So what are you doing here?"

"Well it's a long story. My girl pal here, Megan Winter" — he paused and put his hand on Megan's shoulder — "is not just a pretty face, she's also a hugely talented designer. You may have seen her on TV."

Zane studied Megan. "Er, no."

"Well you will. She's going places, giving your neighbours Prada and the likes a run for their money when it comes to shoes."

Megan felt a flush rise on her cheeks. That was always the way when Brendon started singing her praises. He liked to gush, and while that was very sweet, it could also be a little embarrassing.

"Not shoes like these." Brendon took the shoe Megan held. "Shoes that sparkle, shoes that make the wearer feel a million dollars, like they can achieve anything. Even the soles are elegant and bespoke."

"Though these are very nice too," Megan said, pointing at the ivy shoes.

"Well that all sounds lovely, and congratulations on your success," Zane said, directing his attention back to Brendon. "Do your girl pal's shoes have a website?"

"Absolutely." Brendon pulled out his wallet, flipped it open and produced a Winter Shoes business card. "Here."

Zane studied it and swiped his tongue over his bottom lip. "So is this your phone number on here, Brendon?"

"No, it's mine," Megan said. "Call me anytime if you'd like to see some samples."

"Yes, we're looking for shelf space," Brendon said.

"We?" Zane let his gaze drift over Brendon, from his toes to his face. "How does that work?"

Megan suppressed a smile — she could spot admiration a mile off. It looked like Zane thought Brendon was as cute as Brendon thought Zane was, and why not, they'd make a handsome couple.

"Yes, we. I'm her PR manager," Brendon said, jutting out his hip and smiling.

"In that case, I'd better have your number too." Zane handed the card back to Brendon. "I'll get you a pen." He turned and headed to the till.

Megan poked Brendon in the ribs. "He likes you," she mouthed.

"Shh, play it cool." Brendon pressed his index finger to his lips but quickly dropped it when Zane appeared around the flowers again.

"Here," Zane said, handing over a pink pen that appeared to be studded with diamonds.

Brendon quickly added his mobile number to the back of the card.

"So have you been all business, business, business, or have you been seeing the sights?" Zane asked as Brendon handed over his contact details.

"We've been up to the Hollywood sign," Brendon said, "but we only arrived yesterday so just getting started."

"We intend to hit the beach later," Megan added.

"Where are you staying?"

"Santa Monica, and it's—"

Brendon was interrupted by wild yapping. A bundle of pale brown fur appeared from behind the till, with a white, jewel-encrusted lead dragging behind it.

"Dolce, what are you doing, you bad girl," Zane said, stooping to gather up the excited dog. "Sorry, she's got a way of getting the knot undone, I don't know how she does it. She's supposed to stay behind the till."

"Oh, she is so adorable," Brendon said, stroking Dolce's head. She licked him wildly, her little pink tongue frantic to touch as much of his hand as possible. "I've got a Pomeranian too. Called Gucci."

"No freaking way," Zane said, his eyes widening. "Boy or girl?"

"Boy, and sex mad, humps anything." Brendon laughed.

Zane laughed too, his gaze not shifting from Brendon.

Megan moved away, her attention caught by a collection of ankle boots that had the toes cut out. They were in a variety of primary colours and some had wedges. She'd leave the boys to their flirting and investigate the competition. It would be so cool, super-cool to have her designs in LA Hype—the stuff of dreams. She'd have the table in the middle of the shop and this first shelf, the one people would gravitate naturally towards when they came into the shop.

After a few minutes she felt Brendon at her side. "Are we good to go?" she asked. "Finished chatting?"

"Yes, though it is absolutely dreamy in here." He sighed.

Megan got the feeling he was talking about more than just the shop. "Perhaps it is time to hit the beach and find ourselves a cocktail to sip."

"I like your way of thinking."

They headed to the door. Brendon pulled it open and the summer heat flooded in.

"Bye, Zane," Brendon called.

"Yep, catch you around, Brendon, and I'll check up on that space thing, drop you a bell."

"Appreciate it."

The door shut behind them.

"What space thing?" Megan asked.

Brendon put his arm around her waist and tugged her close as they strode by Prada. "Zane is only the goddamn manager of LA Hype now."

"Wow, that's great for him."

"And great for us."

"Why?"

"Because it means he gets some sway in what products are stocked and how they're displayed."

Megan felt her heart rate triple. She stopped and turned to Brendon. "No way."

"Yes, way. He might just—and it's only a might at this point in time—be able to get Winter Shoes some shelf space."

"Bloody hell." Megan clapped her hand over her mouth. She stared at Brendon.

"Are you happy or what?"

"More than happy. That would be amazing." She paused. "Really? I'm not dreaming, am I?"

He pinched her arm.

"Oww." She rubbed the sore spot.

"Nope, not dreaming." Brendon did a little jig on the spot then stilled and glanced around. He smoothed his hair and squared his shoulders. "It's very real. And once he sees the product, I can't imagine for a minute he won't snap up your designs. They'll sell like hot cakes."

"You think?" Megan's knees felt a little weak, she had fluttery butterflies in her belly. She'd only been dreaming of having her product in LA Hype a few minutes ago, and now, now her clever, smooth-talking bestie might be about to make it happen.

"You've gone pale," Brendon said. "Which is so not a good look here." He held out the crook of his arm for her to take. "And I guess we'll be needing a more permanent address."

Megan slipped her hand through his arm. "Why?"

"Because if we've achieved this in just the first morning when we're jet-lagged and tired from hiking, imagine what we can do in a month, sweetpea."

3

"Gucci, you're going to love it here," Brendon said, placing his excitable dog on the long winding path that ran from Santa Monica down past Muscle Beach, onto Venice Beach and beyond. "But just watch out for skaters and boarders, okay, they might not see you."

As he'd spoken, a woman with long, thin legs, tiny denim shorts and a cropped top speed-skated past. She held her iPhone and the headphones were in place. She stared straight ahead managing to look elegant and cool, and as though skating was effortless.

Gucci span in a circle and started barking. He wrapped his blue velvet lead around Brendon's legs and tangled himself up at the same time.

"Oh for goodness sake," Brendon muttered, unclipping him and stepping out of the muddle. "I only put you down for a second."

"Maybe we should carry him a little way first, get out of this bit, it's always busy by these restaurants." Having been in Santa Monica for nearly a week now, Megan and Brendon were beginning to get their bearings as well as having adjusted to LA time. The only problem was that staying in Bay Place was starting to eat at their bank balances, and they were now paying extra to have Gucci with them.

"Good idea," Brendon said. He stepped backwards to avoid a handsome young skater who, like most of the boys on wheels, was topless. Brendon's excitement had dulled a little and he didn't feel the need to take a photo of every one that went past. He did still give the boarder an appreciative glance, though.

They ambled along, Megan enjoying the slight breeze that wafted in from the sea. The constant rumble of the waves had also become familiar. Megan was loving being so close to the ocean. She'd even ventured for several swims when the waves hadn't been too choppy. She'd found, however, that when she'd been swimming along, quietly, her mind had drifted to thoughts of James. He was never far from her thoughts. Their time together, albeit brief, had imprinted itself on her soul. It had felt so right, as if they'd been searching for each other then had finally met. Like two magnets drawn to each other, or two halves of a star connecting.

But what was the point in such fanciful thinking? They were over. She'd never see him again.

"Right, now behave." Brendon placed Gucci on the wide sandy pavement. There was no one around for him to immediately get excited by and he luckily stayed calm. "Right this way, Gucci-baby," Brendon said. "We're going to go check out Muscle Beach, there's always lots going on there."

"We'll get an ice cream, shall we?" Megan said, glancing at two teenage boys who were eating huge ice cream cones sprinkled with sweets. "And sit on those big benches in the shade just along from the weights."

"Good plan."

Gucci trotted along, his little tongue hanging out and his tail upright. He was scanning the area, taking in the sounds and smells. It was good to have him with them and he'd coped admirably with the flight.

"I think it would be love at first sight if he met Dolce, don't you?" Brendon said.

"Oh yes, I can hear doggy wedding bells already." Megan giggled.

Brendon sighed.

"Don't worry, Zane will call, I'm sure he will," Megan said. "It's probably just taking a while for him to organise everything."

"I know, but…it wasn't just about shelf space. I was hoping he'd call just to, you know, chat."

"Likely he wants to be able to answer your questions about the shop and if he can take an order for my shoes."

"I wish he didn't feel like that." Brendon frowned. "Not that getting Winter Shoes into LA Hype isn't terribly important to me. It is, it's just that I thought for old times' sake, being two Brits in town, that we'd get together. He had suggested we go down to Newport Beach for something to eat and to watch the sunset."

"That sounds romantic."

"Only if it bloody happens," Brendon huffed.

"It's only been a few days. Relax, he's likely been rushed off his feet at work."

"I don't think it's that kind of shop."

"Well, let's hope it is if I do get shoes in there."

"Darling, Winter Shoes in there will likely put it on the map." Brendon grinned and gestured ahead. "And what a place on the map to be." Even hanging on hoping for a phone call and a date couldn't detract from his evident pleasure at walking his dog down the long boardwalk, people watching, breathing the sea air and looking forward to an ice cream, which Gucci would likely eat a good portion of.

Before long they came across the area known as Muscle Beach. It was a cordoned-off small rectangular park with a soft tarmac floor and heavy black weights. Huge men and a few beefy women hung about with serious expressions on their faces, skimpy workout clothes on, and tight muscles bulging.

Megan wondered if they worked out in private until they looked so butch — it wouldn't do to start training with a puny body and an LA audience. She watched a man with rippling biceps and straining muscles in his neck bench-press an impossibly heavy-looking set of weights. Another man stood behind him, hands at the ready to help if he struggled. The man behind reminded Megan of James. Not in body — James was tall, lean and athletic — but he had the same soft dark hair and brooding expression. His eyes were black and he had a peppering of stubble. He glanced up, caught Megan's eye and a dazzling white smile crossed his lips.

She didn't smile back, instead she looked away. It hurt that he wasn't James, not that it was his fault he wasn't the man she'd left behind, but still, she couldn't quite bring herself to smile at him.

"You have an admirer," Brendon said, elbowing her.

"Mmm..."

"You gonna say hi?"

"No, I..." She twisted then rested her back on the fence that circled the gym area and faced the ice cream parlour.

"What?"

"I'm not ready for any of that. I wish..."

Brendon placed his hand on her shoulder. "You wish that it hadn't ended with James, I know, but you'll have to move on at some point, and by the grace of God, a hunk from Muscle Beach would see you right."

"But—"

"No buts, you should go and talk to him."

"I'm not sure." She wouldn't know what to say. Conversation had come so easily with James—they'd had lots in common and a similar sense of humour. He'd been interested in her and she'd been fascinated by him. What would she say to a shiny, big American guy who spent his days posing for passers-by?

"Of course you're sure. You have to get back in the dating saddle at some point and at the moment, chances are it will be an American guy. Go for it. Put your foot in the stirrup and hop up. Look he's coming over."

Megan pulled in a deep breath. Brendon was right of course, she needed to get over James and allow herself to at least explore a new relationship even if it wasn't with 'the one'.

She turned around, set a smile on her lips and watched the big bloke she'd thought had a similar face to James walk right on past her.

Two girls in matching denim shorts and bikini tops stood to her left. With their hair in identical plaits, they appeared to be twins.

Buff Guy swaggered up to them and nudged his hip against the rail, his back facing Megan and Brendon. The girls giggled and nudged each other before sparking a conversation with him.

"Snooze you lose," Brendon said with a tut.

"I'm really not bothered I lost," Megan said, again spinning away from the pumped-up bodies in front of her. "Come on, let's go get that ice cream and find some shade."

"Good idea. Come on, Gucci, this way, ice-creamy time."

Within a few minutes, Megan held an enormous tub of ice cream coated in strawberry sauce and sprinkled with tiny white chocolate drops and crushed meringue — bliss in a tub.

"Over there," Brendon said, "where we sat the other day, it was quiet and shady."

"Yes, that was nice." Megan headed towards the cluster of palm trees that was set back from the path and sheltered from the wind. Four benches, made of dark wood, were set in the shade. One was occupied by a man with scruffy blond hair reading from a sheaf of papers and eating from a huge bag of crisps.

"Come on, Gucci, I have treats for you," Brendon said, tugging Gucci away from a particularly delicious smelling lamp post. "This way."

Megan sat, glad to take the weight off her feet. A sweet treat, a view of the ocean and the shade of a tree were just what she needed.

Gucci jumped onto the bench and placed his little paws on Brendon's thigh, his neck straining for the first chocolate drop.

"Oh, here you go," Brendon said, giving him one. "You're so demanding."

Gucci gobbled it up then let out a couple of sharp barks and tried to get down.

Brendon tutted. "Well don't go far." He unclipped the lead. "Stay near Daddy."

Gucci jumped down and headed straight for the man with the crisps.

"Bloody hell," Brendon muttered. "I knew it was a mistake to trust him."

"I'll grab him. Hold this." Megan passed her ice cream to Brendon.

She wandered across the patch of sun-withered grass. "Gucci, come on, over here, you little rascal."

Gucci ignored her and jumped onto the bench next to the man, disturbing him from his reading.

"Oh, bloody hell. I'm so sorry," Megan said, mortified as Gucci put his paws on the guy's leg and poked his head deep into the crisp packet. She reached for him and scooped his wriggling body into her arms. The crisps toppled to the floor and spilt onto the parched grass. "I really am terribly sorry," she said again. "So sorry."

"It's fine." The man looked up. He had piercing blue eyes the colour of sapphires, perfect tanned skin and his hair, although scruffy, appeared in tip-top soft condition and was carefully trimmed around his ears and neck. He wore a plain white T-shirt, worn jeans with a tear on the left knee and around his right wrist, several leather bands were twisted together.

Megan stared at him. He was one of the most handsome men she'd ever seen.

He tipped his head and studied her. "Do you have a pen?"

"Er no, sorry."

He shrugged. "Well I don't either, so I'm afraid I can't give you my autograph."

"Autograph." Megan frowned in confusion. "Why on earth would I want your autograph?"

He continued to stare at her, his eyes flashing in the sunlight. "You're British right?"

"Yes, I'm from London."

"And you don't know who I am?"

"No, should I?" Megan switched Gucci in her embrace. This was turning into a weird conversation.

He put his head back and laughed. "No, not at all. Just not many people I meet around here don't know who I am."

"And that's funny because…?"

"Because it's a refreshing change." He set down his papers and stood. "Tate Simmons, nice to meet you."

"Oh, okay, well I'm Megan Winter and this little bugger is Gucci. My friend over there is Brendon."

He smiled and held up his hand to Brendon.

Brendon took that as a sign to come over. "I'm really truly sorry about Gucci going after your crisps." He bent to pick them up, shoving his bum in the air.

"Crisps…ahh the chips, don't worry, it's no big deal," Tate said. "I shouldn't have been eating trash anyway."

"I'll buy you some more," Brendon offered.

"No, forget it." Tate flapped his hand in the air. "Though you could maybe help me out with something."

"Sure." Brendon smiled and licked his lips. "Anything you want."

Megan groaned inwardly. Her gaydar was telling her that Tate Simmons didn't have a gay bone in his body, but that still didn't stop Brendon flirting.

"I'm learning these lines, I start a new movie in a few weeks—"

"Oh are you an actor?" Brendon asked, his eyes widening.

"Er, yeah."

"Would we have seen anything you're in?" Brendon appeared beyond excited. "Anything at all?"

"Well I guess not, if you don't recognise me." Tate glanced from Brendon to Megan and smiled. "But this movie coming up is big and it will be my first lead role as a British character." He sat and picked up his papers. A slight breeze ruffled his hair, and Megan wondered what it would be like to run her fingers through it.

There was a small tightening in her belly. It was too soon to think of running her fingers through another man's hair.

It only felt like a heartbeat since she'd been stroking James' hair, caressing him, kissing him, lying in bed with him…

"And I could really do with some input on the accent." Tate shrugged.

Brendon passed Megan her ice cream and took Gucci from her. He put him back on his lead. "Well, we could help," he said seriously. "If you'd like?"

"I would really appreciate it. I've got a voice coach, and she's nice and all, but she's gone through it several times and I'm still not quite there." Again he looked at Megan. He narrowed his eyes and tipped his head. "What do you think?"

Nope, Megan thought, not a flicker of interest in Brendon. This handsome man wanted her input and not her gay best friend's. But perhaps that was fine, maybe a bit of time with Tate might just make her think about getting back in the saddle, even if she wasn't quite ready to put her foot in the stirrup yet and hop up.

"Okay, what are you stuck with?" She took a seat next to him and popped in a spoonful of her ice cream that was starting to melt.

"Well, I'm trying to go for the Hugh Grant plum-in-the-mouth style, that's what my coach says." Tate chuckled. "Because it suits Lord Butler, that's the character I play." He'd put the accent on for the last few words.

"Not bad," Brendon said, sitting on the other side of Tate and peering at the script.

"Thanks, but this word, squirrel, how do you guys say that?" He pointed to a line and angled it towards Megan.

"There's been a squirrel in the pantry again, someone needs to take care of it," she read aloud.

"See you say it perfectly, squirrel, squirrel." Tate tutted. He hadn't got it right.

"You're not saying the 'e'," Megan said with a smile. "Squirrel." She emphasised the last syllable.

"Squirrel," Brendon repeated.

"Squirrel," Tate said, his brow creasing into a frown of

concentration. "There's been a squirrel in the pantry again, someone needs to take care of it."

"That's better," Megan said, scooping up a particularly gooey bit of strawberry sauce and licking it off the spoon.

Tate watched her. "Is that nice?"

"Fab. I love ice cream."

He smiled. "Don't see many women around here eating the stuff."

"Why not?"

"They're all obsessed with calories." His gaze drifted down her body. "Clearly not something you have to worry about."

A tingle travelled up Megan's spine and her cheeks flushed a little at the compliment.

"Where are you guys staying?" Tate glanced at Brendon.

"Bay Place Hotel." Brendon said, nodding towards the way they'd come.

"Ah, yes, up by the pier."

"That's the one," Megan said. "It's lovely."

"But a bit pricey and we're hoping to stay in LA for several more weeks," Brendon said.

"Oh, are you?" Tate turned back to Megan. "Why's that then?"

"Well it started out as a bit of a holiday, but I run my own designer-shoe business and —"

"Winter Shoes," Brendon added. "*The* name to be seen in on the red carpet, if you're a woman that is."

"Nice," Tate said. "Good for you."

"Thanks, and I'm hoping to maybe get some sales up on Rodeo Drive, spread the word about my designs over here and get a few celebs endorsing them."

"And you need somewhere to stay more suitable for a long visit." Tate nodded seriously.

"In a nutshell." Megan nodded.

"Nutshell?" Tate looked confused.

"You know, what squirrels eat." She laughed.

Tate laughed too. "What *squirrels* eat."

"Yay, you got it." Megan grinned at him. Damn, the guy was gorgeous, sinfully gorgeous. He no doubt had an army of female Tate Simmons fans.

"I might be able to help you guys out," Tate said. "My mate's got a place in Venice Beach that he wants to let out while he's travelling in Malaysia for a couple of months. It's empty now."

"Really? That would be great," Megan said.

"Venice Beach, oh what a damn fine address," Brendon stood, and Gucci immediately started yapping around his ankles.

"Wanna go have a look?" Tate said. "It's not far from here."

"But do you have a key?" Brendon asked.

"It's with the neighbour. Dirk headed off last week but he's still hoping for a renter, asked me and a few of our other mates to keep an eye out."

"Well that renter could be us," Megan said, standing. "Don't you think, Brendon?"

"Yes, just what we need. Lead the way, fine fellow." Brendon made a sweeping gesture with his hand.

Tate smiled and looked at Megan. "It's got two bedrooms."

"Great." Brendon tugged Gucci's lead. "I won't have to listen to her snoring anymore. The hotel room is killing me. She looks like all your dreams wrapped up in a fantasy and sprinkled with rainbow dust, but this girl snores like a hound from Hell."

"Brendon!" Megan said both shocked and embarrassed. "I do not."

"How do you know?" Brendon winked and grinned. "You're asleep."

"Don't worry, Megan," Tate said, resting his hand on her arm. "I don't believe everything I hear about people. That's how you have to be when you're as famous as me. There's always gossip about me and what I'm supposedly doing but I let it all pass me by."

'As famous as me.' How famous? Megan wondered. Maybe

41

he did look a little familiar.

"This way," Tate said, walking at her side. He steered them onto a path that led into the houses rather than back to the beach.

Megan decided that she'd have to Google their new friend later. She glanced at Brendon several steps ahead. He was on his iPhone. She sighed. She'd bet her best diamanté mules that he was Googling Tate Simmons right now.

"So do you start this movie soon?" Megan asked as they ambled past a canal that had two-storey homes flanking its sides.

"Yes, in a few weeks. Got to finish off something else first, a fly on the wall thing about the life guards in LA. Audiences have been fascinated by that subject matter since *Baywatch*. All those studs and gorgeous beach babes running in slow motion up and down the beach wearing hardly anything at all."

"I suppose so, and I bet it's nice working outdoors, by the ocean."

"Yeah, I love it. Plus I get to go out and surf a bit too."

"You like doing that?"

"Yeah, I adore surfing. Did a movie a few years ago about a surfer who made it all the way to the top, won the World Surfing Championships. Was cool to be filming something I loved so much."

Now that sounded familiar. Megan wondered if she'd actually seen that film, or certainly heard about it. Hadn't Georgie watched it on a plane and gone on and on about the hunky lead who bared his chest throughout the entire movie? "So no filming today?" she asked.

"No." He pointed to the right. "This way."

Megan followed him. It was such a pretty area, all the homes appeared loved and the warren of canals were adorable. She could see why the area got its name from Venice.

"We've had a week of filming," Tate said. "Damn director went on a bender, hasn't been seen for days. New guy took over a few days ago. He's been going through what we've done so far in edits apparently, and we're due on set tomorrow to pick up where we left off."

"Gosh, sorry about the disruption."

"Doesn't matter." He turned and gave her full-wattage grin. "I wouldn't have met a pretty British girl if that hadn't happened." He'd spoken with a near perfect English accent.

Megan looked up at him. It was hard to resist him when he wasn't smiling, but with his grin directed at her, it was damn near impossible.

"And we're here." He nodded over his shoulder. "It's this one."

"Wow," Brendon said, tucking his phone away.

"Wow indeed. I don't think we'll be able to afford this." Megan shook her head. Just when she'd thought they might have struck lucky, too.

A two-storey home with a neat front garden, deep porch and wide windows stood before them. It was attached to the house next door and both were painted a soft cream with sandy-coloured roof tiles.

"Ah, he only wants enough to cover bills and maintenance, it will be fine. Dirk isn't exactly on the breadline," Tate said. "Wait here and I'll get the key."

Tate slipped into the messy garden next door and was quickly hidden by foliage. It seemed they weren't keen gardeners and the tall fronds of plants Megan didn't recognise had taken over.

"This would be an awesome place to stay," Brendon said, linking his arm with Megan's.

"I know, talk about falling on our feet."

"Or rather fate smiling sweetly on us in the shape of the most beautiful man I have ever laid eyes on." He performed a lavish swoon, wiping his wrist over his forehead and allowing his knees to sag.

"He is very handsome."

"Handsome doesn't begin to start the description. He's a Grecian god, a man to be worshipped and adored, he should be selling his seed for millions like they do with stallions."

Megan giggled. "Shut up."

"No I won't shut up. I just Googled him."

"I knew you were doing that and I wish you wouldn't. It's so uncool."

"Well I'm glad I did. He's got over three million Twitter followers, he's the star of a big crime series over here that shows on Vixen as well as having lead roles in two movies in the last three years. The guy is seriously famous."

"I've never heard of him."

"Well that doesn't mean that millions haven't. He's also rumoured to be the new face of Armani."

"I can see how that would work."

"Got it." Tate appeared holding up a key. "And I called Dirk, he said it's yours for two hundred dollars a week."

"Blimey O'Riley," Brendon said. "We'll take it, we're paying that a night."

Tate laughed. "Blimey O'Riley, I love how you folk speak." He waggled the key. "Wanna look around?"

"Sure." Megan took a deep breath and followed Tate. Everything felt right about the sweet little home. The neat path, the orange flowers in a tub by the front door that had busy bees scrambling for pollen, the large window that was being gently stroked by the fronds of a squat palm tree.

Tate opened the door, and they stepped in. Brendon let Gucci off his lead so he could run around and explore, which he did, punctuated by excited barking.

"Two bedrooms and a bathroom upstairs," Tate said, "then two rooms down here. That one has a fireplace and TV, the other a table and sofa bed and then there's the kitchen."

"It's lovely, and it smells so clean," Megan said.

"Dirk is a neat freak." Tate shrugged.

"Well good, because so am I," Brendon said as he pointed up the stairs. "I'll go check it out."

"Pick the best bedroom, more like," Megan said with a

smile.

"For you, dearest, I'll pick the best bedroom for you." He went up the narrow flight at a jog.

"Come and see the kitchen," Tate said.

Megan followed him down the short corridor. He had wide shoulders and a long back. His butt was showcased perfectly in his slightly loose denims that had one pocket fashionably frayed. She wondered if he had a girlfriend. Who was she kidding? Of course he did. He likely had a string of supermodels and actresses at his beck and call.

"What do you think?" he asked as they stepped into the kitchen.

"Oh it's lovely." And it was, all white cupboards with chrome appliances, set against bright orange wall tiles. The wide window looked out onto a pretty terrace with a trailing rose over a pagoda and a wrought-iron set of garden furniture with orange cushions.

"It will be sufficient for you?" he asked, stepping up close.

"More than sufficient. I think it's safe to say we'll take it." Megan breathed in deeply — she could smell Tate's aftershave now. It was tangy and citrusy, maybe with a hint of pepper.

"Good, then it is only a phone call. If you give me your number, I'll forward you Dirk's and you can go from there." He pushed his fingers through his fringe, which flopped back into the exact same position, and smiled.

Damn, the guy knew how cute he was. She'd bet he used his charm and good looks to get anything he wanted in life. To breeze through things mere mortals had to battle to succeed in.

"Hell of a way to get a number from a girl," she said then laughed. As if he'd really want her number? It was a business arrangement, nothing more.

"I'm inventive, sure." He grinned and his eyes sparkled. "And determined."

Determined to what?

Megan pulled out her phone and read out her number. He

tapped it into his then her phone beeped as Dirk's contact details arrived.

"There, you're all set." Tate put his phone away.

"Thank you, like seriously, much appreciated." Megan studied the way his eyelashes curled and how his eyebrows were perfectly neat. "Happy to give a few more English accent lessons as payment."

"Well that would be cool." He stepped a little closer, his body heat pouring onto her. "But..."

"But what?" she asked quietly.

He tucked a lock of her hair behind her ear and dipped his head.

Her skin tingled where he'd touched her. His eyes were like an invitation to dive into a glorious deep pool of water. There was something hypnotic about him, magnetic.

James.

She pulled in a breath. Brendon was right, she had to move on, even if she wasn't quite in the zone to, and who better than a gorgeous celeb who smelt so divine?

"There is something else you could do, if you really want to say thank you," he said in a low murmuring voice.

She swallowed. She hardly knew this guy, maybe he'd ask for... No he didn't seem the type to come on so strong. But she was in a strange land, surrounded by foreigners and she was a long way from home.

"There's this little award thing coming up," he said. "I need a date and not someone I've co-starred with or a singer—God, that went wrong last time—crazy chick, or anyone majorly in the public eye. A pretty English rose like you would be perfect, if you fancy it."

"An award thing?" Megan's head was spinning. Had he really just asked her out on a date? Not any old date for a beer and pizza, but to attend an award ceremony?

"Yes, it's only small, in LA luckily, so no travelling. I reckon you and I could rock the red carpet. We'd be cute together."

"Red carpet?"

"Only if you want to." He gave a confident smile. "No pressure. I get that we just met, but it's the way I roll. I go with the flow, do what feels right, take what looks good."

Oh but he had a right to be confident. Megan's insides were swirling and her knees felt like they didn't quite belong to her—the red carpet, a date with this beautiful man, an actual real LA award ceremony where she'd be a guest.

"Well that sounds, er…"

"Perfect, lovely…?" he asked tipping his eyebrows. "Like the best type of fun ever?"

"All of those. Yes." She smiled up at him. "I'd love to come with you."

4

Tate pressed a chaste kiss to Megan's cheek then stepped away. "I'll call you, tomorrow, sort out the details."

"When is it, the award ceremony?"

"Week on Saturday." He threw over his shoulder as he headed to the hallway, "Speak tomorrow, and call Dirk ASAP to let him know you want the place. It'll get him off my back asking about it."

"Okay. Will do." She watched him go and heard the front door click shut.

Bloody hell. What would she wear? What shoes would be best? Tate was tall, like James, so she could wear her highest heels. Damn, why was she comparing him to James? She couldn't do that. James wasn't in her life now. Instead, she had a hot Hollywood actor wooing her.

"Oh my, oh my, oh my…" Brendon rushed into the kitchen, Gucci racing alongside him in a half-skip, half-run. "Guess what?" He gripped Megan's forearms.

"No, you guess what!"

"What?"

"You go first."

"No you…"

"No you…"

"Both say it," he said. "One, two three."

"Tate just asked me to go a red carpet award ceremony with him next week."

"Zane just called, we're going on a date and you have shelf space at LA Hype."

They both froze and stared at each other.

"What?" Brendon said, his eyes wide. "Really?"

"Zane called? You're going out, that's great." Megan's heart soared — she was so happy for Brendon. *And I have shelf space!*

"Yes, can't wait. And you've got shelf space, sweetpea. Not just shelf space, he's planning on a big launch party to present you to Rodeo Drive. He and his senior managers are in love and lust with Winter Shoes, they want to help make you the next big thing and the sooner the better, they're not hanging around on this one."

"Oh wow…" Megan spotted a bar stool pushed under the granite counter. She pulled it out and sat down. "That's incredible, I mean I hoped, dared to dream, but…"

"But it's really happening. We're to go first thing in the morning and hash through the details. They love your website, your designs, the whole brand and those stints on *Rupert and Jayne* did your profile the world of good. You'll need to call Enid today and make sure a container of product is sent out. We've got some samples but you're going to need more."

"Yes…" Megan said then grinned. "So you're off to Newport Beach with hunky Zane, eh?"

Brendon clasped his hands beneath his chin. "Yes, oh yes, I am so excited. We're going on Saturday because he's off the next day if we have a late night and he's tired, you know." Brendon winked. Suddenly his face changed. "What? Rewind to Tate Simmons. You're going to an *award* ceremony with our new best actor buddy? How the hell did that come about?" He pulled out the other bar stool and sat.

"He just asked. Came right out with it. Said he didn't have a date, didn't want an actress or a crazy chick and would I go with him. I guess I'm an unknown in his world, so won't detract attention from him."

"I'll say you will. You scrub up pretty well you know, or had you forgotten as it's so long since you dolled up." He paused. "Blimey, what are you going to wear?"

She shook her head. "No idea, I didn't bring any fancy dresses. I didn't think I'd need them."

Brendon clapped then rubbed his hands together. "That's okay because we're going to LA Hype tomorrow, we'll get you something there."

"I can't afford that."

"You won't have to." He nodded slowly and tapped the end of his nose. "I think a loan might be possible."

Megan reached out and pulled Brendon into a hug. "I can't believe all this is happening. It's such a roller coaster. A new place to live, Winter Shoes flying high, new men in our lives."

"Yeah, baby, hang on for the ride 'cause we're only just getting started. The world is our oyster and the city is ours to conquer."

"Georgie, I can't talk long because we're heading up to Beverley Hills," Megan said excitedly, "but I've got to fill you in on what's going on."

"Oh get you, Beverly Hills. Not so long ago you were catching the Tube and coping with the London drizzle like those you've left behind."

"You could always come out for a holiday, we've got a place to stay now in Venice Beach. I'll text you the address. It's beautiful and much cheaper than the hotel, plus there's space for you to stay, have your own room downstairs."

"Well I might just do that."

"I'd love it if you did. I've got something big happening and it would be cool to have you by my side, but I understand if you can't, you've got big things happening too, what with the wedding and planning and work and Tom and —"

"Megan, stop, tell me. What is this big thing you've got happening? I'm dying of suspense here."

"Oh yes, that. It's why we're going to Beverley Hills. Brendon is cosy with the manager at LA Hype, a boutique on Rodeo Drive, and I've got shelf space for Winter Shoes. They're going all out, I'm having a launch party and everything."

"A launch party. When?"

"Soon, next week maybe."

"It's your birthday next week."

"Oh yes, I'd forgotten. So much is going on." Megan giggled.

"I'd say. Have you spoken to Enid? Is she coping with all of this?"

"Yes, she's a star. She's speed sending a bunch of shoes in all sizes out today. She worked late last night to get it organised. If there's going to be a launch there needs to be product for people to buy.

"She is great, on the ball. She gets it. I knew she'd make a difference to your life."

"She really has. I'll give her a raise as soon as I start pulling in some more revenue. She's allowed me to free up my time for pursuing new ventures, growing Winter Shoes, enterprise and innovation. I've still got designs to work on too."

"This is so exciting." Georgie paused. "What about James? Have you heard from him?"

Just hearing his name set a lump of lead in Megan's belly. They could have been so good together. They *had* been so good together. "No, not a word. I screwed that up big time. Or rather Dylan did."

"I heard that Dylan's not doing great. He's lost his job."

"Shit, has he?"

"Yeah, Tom saw Sean who said Dylan just hadn't been turning up."

"What an idiot, he needs the money."

"Maybe he'll come to his senses."

"I hope so, because he still seems to think we have a future, which we definitely don't."

"Well I know that, and so does everyone else. Tom says he's deluded, though."

"That would sum it up."

"So…" Georgie said, stringing out the word. "Are there any hunky LA guys who've caught your attention?"

Megan paused. Was it too soon to mention Tate? No, who was she kidding? If she didn't and Brendon told Georgie first she'd be furious. "Well there is this one cute bloke."

"Oh, do tell."

"He's the one that set us up with the house in Venice Beach."

"What is he? An estate agent or something?"

"No, he's an actor."

"Isn't everyone in LA?" Georgie laughed.

"Yeah, I guess." Megan hesitated.

"What?"

"Nothing."

"I know you too well, Megan Rose Winter. What's going on? Is he like *famous* famous?"

"I think you might have seen one of his movies." Megan frowned as she recalled the name of it — Brendon had been talking about it the evening before. "*Riding the Crest*, I think it was called."

"Oh my God, you have not seriously been hanging out with Tate Simmons, he's like my top crush of last year, well after Zac Efron and Chris Hemsworth that is."

"I didn't know you were such a fan."

"What's not to love? I watched that film three times, not because of the intricate plot or the flawless acting but because that guy is hotter than the sun."

"Well yeah, he is very handsome."

"And Brendon is gnawing off his toes because there is no way Tate Simmons swings both ways is there?"

"No, I think you're right. Brendon did his best flirt moves but nothing."

"So are you going out on a date?"

"Yes, we're off to an award ceremony next week, a red carpet thing."

Georgie wailed and Megan held the phone away from her ear.

"It must be The Sparkling Stars Awards. I cannot believe I'm not there," Georgie cried. "All this happening and I'm stuck in the office in London and it's raining when it should be sunny."

"But you have the wedding to plan. That's exciting."

"Yes, of course it is, and I can't wait, but seriously, you're going out with Tate Simmons in LA and will be on the red carpet and I'm not there to supervise the whole thing. You're having a launch party on Rodeo Drive with no doubt oodles of champagne and delicious morsels to nibble on."

Megan laughed. "So come over. I'd love to have you here."

Georgie hesitated. "It's the cost, to be honest, what with the wedding and everything…"

Megan pulled in deep breath. She was missing Georgie already. What they had was special. Their bond was strong and they always shared major life events. "I understand. Really I do."

"I know." Georgie was quiet for a moment. "So what's he like, Tate Simmons?"

"Gorgeous obviously."

"Yep."

"And with a smile that's insanely beautiful and confident and also a bit well…"

"What?"

"I dunno, he's so confident he's almost cocky."

"What do you mean?"

"Well he was pretty damn sure I'd say yes to going to this event with him."

"Well duh, what girl in their right mind wouldn't?"

"I get your point but…"

"Tell me, Megan."

"But well, I do still like James. I can't just switch that off, you know, he was starting to settle in my heart."

"I know, sweetie, but who better on the face of the planet to rebound on than Tate I-want-to-lick-him-all-over Simmons."

"Hey, that's my date." Megan laughed. Georgie always made her feel better.

"Well make sure you get a lick in on my behalf."

"I'm not making any licking promises of any kind."

"That's a shame. Listen, I've got a stack of emails to catch up on before everyone heads home for the day. You have a great time and don't make a move without letting me know all the details."

"I won't, I promise. Take care." Megan hung up.

Georgie was certainly excited about her date with an A-lister, as Megan had known she would be. But was Tate just a pretty face? He'd seemed fun and charming and had said all the right things. But did he have the depths of character that James had? Would Tate fight for what he believed in even if it meant risking his reputation, his life? Would Tate inspire her to want to be a better person, to reach for her goals?

She didn't know the answers to her own questions, and she wouldn't until she gave him a chance. She needed to get to know him a bit better. Find out if he had the qualities she knew she wanted in the man in her life. The last thing she wanted was another Dylan, a guy who wouldn't let her breathe without his permission, but equally she'd didn't want someone without substance. A pretty face wouldn't be enough to keep her happy and satisfied for all eternity.

"Well, well, well, if it isn't the star of the show, or should I say star of the shoes?" Zane reached for Megan and pulled her into a hug. "You have us all at LA Hype in quite a tizz of excitement, you know."

Megan grinned over his shoulder at Brendon, who was fussing with his hair. "Thank you, it is very exciting."

"Indeed. Your designs have just blown us away." Zane held her at arm's length and shook his head. "Such a pretty little thing and so clever too."

"I'm just doing what I love and that's designing shoes."

"Well your shoes are the best. We have been stuck in a rut

of flowery designs for too many seasons now. It's time to have some sparkle back in the window."

"There's a consignment of stock on the way," Brendon said. "Should be here within forty-eight hours."

"Great news." Zane released Megan and turned to Brendon. "I'm planning for next week. We don't hang around here. I don't want other shops snapping up Winter Shoes first and saying they're exclusive. I know we can't be your only stockist, Megan, but we can be your first."

"That suits me." She couldn't believe her luck, it was perfect. "What day were you thinking?"

"The fifteenth."

"Oh, your birthday," Brendon said, clasping her hand. "How amazing is that?"

"Well it certainly makes for an amazing birthday present, to be getting shelf space here."

"It's no less than you deserve," Zane said. "I get the feeling you're going places, and if LA Hype can help you, then we want to do all that we can."

"That's so kind of you."

"Nothing kind about it. We recognise talent."

"Here, here," Brendon said. He then walked over to a rail holding floor-length dresses. "There is one other thing?"

"Oh, what's that?" Zane asked, putting his hands on his hips and making no secret of the fact he was surveying Brendon from his toes to the top of his head.

"Our Megan here has caught the eye of a certain Hollywood actor and she's going on a date."

"Oh…" Zane turned back to Megan with his eyebrows raised. "Who is that then?"

"Well it's kind of for an official engagement, I don't know if it's a date."

"He's asked you to be his date." Brendon frowned. "That makes it a date."

"I suppose."

"Who? Who are you talking about?" Zane asked. He looked about ready to stomp his foot.

"Well..." Brendon was clearly enjoying the suspense. "Our Megan here is going to The Sparkling Stars Awards with Tate Simmons."

"Oh my giddy heart, really?" Zane's eyes widened. "How, I mean, what?"

"They bumped into each other. Megan helped him with his English accent that he's perfecting for his next movie and hey presto, date."

Zane fluttered his hand in front of his face. "That man makes me all aquiver. Oh, he's such a dreamboat, if only he had one single gay cell in his body I'm sure I could turn him, given the chance."

"He doesn't." Brendon plucked out a long white dress and studied it. "He only has eyes for the ladies, and this one in particular."

"Yeah, I heard he'd split up from that Titiana girl, the singer. She's off her rocker." Zane shivered. "She scares me half to death."

"Well yes, but that's okay, you don't need to go anywhere near scary Raven girls." Brendon cast his attention over Zane. "And if you do, I'll protect you."

Zane giggled. "Oh my hero."

"Guys, please," Megan said, laughing. "We have stuff to sort out."

"Yes, you're right," Brendon said, hanging up the white dress and pulling out a long red one with a fishtail hem. "And first things first, you need something to wear on your outing with Tate."

"Of course you do, darling." Zane ran his fingers down the satin fabric. "And you must of course borrow anything you want from LA Hype. The only condition is if you get asked who you're wearing you give us a mention."

"I can easily do that, but I doubt I'll get asked."

"Baby, you'll be on Tate Simmons' arm. Believe you me, you will get asked what you're wearing and so much more."

Megan's heart soared. Wow, she really was hitting the LA scene with a bang. That hadn't gone through her head when she'd agreed to go with Tate. He'd just been an incredibly handsome and persuasive guy asking her out.

"I think you should try this on," Brendon said. "It will suit you perfectly."

"Well it is very lovely." Megan admired the sleek shape and the rich shade of scarlet. "But..."

"Try it on," Zane said. "Go, over there."

"Have we time?" She looked at Brendon.

"Of course. You be doing that while Zane and I work out some extra promo for the launch."

"Okay." Megan headed into the changing room. The dress was heavy on the hanger and already she was wondering which Winter Shoes to wear with it.

"But make sure you show us okay. No trying it on, taking it off then reappearing." Brendon waggled his finger at her.

"Yes, sir," Megan said, pulling the silk curtain up and closing herself into the boutique's changing room.

She tugged off the light summer dress she'd opted for that morning and hung it on the peg. Despite the heat, her makeup had stayed in place and with her hair piled high, her neck was cool.

She checked the price tag on the dress and nearly choked. It was more than the deposit she'd put down on her London apartment a few years previously. It was just as well it was a loan—there was no way she'd splash that much cash on an outfit, no matter how rich she was. Well, maybe one day it would be small change, but until then it was a big dent in the pocket.

The quality of the dress was evident as she slipped it on. The sheer lining was soft and caressed her skin, the fit was exquisite and the way the fishtail fanned out behind her was sexy and fun.

"Well, what do you think?" She stepped out from behind the curtain.

"Oh, my darling, you are a vision of perfection..." Brendon clasped his hand over his mouth.

"I think you'll knock em all dead," Zane said, resting his

hand on Brendon's shoulder. "That dress was made for you, and with your hair and your red lipstick, darling, it's glamour personified."

"You like it then?"

"We love it," Brendon said. "Don't try on any more, nothing will compare."

Megan smiled. A small bubble of excitement popped in her stomach. She'd be wearing this on the red carpet, she'd be surrounded by Hollywood royalty, living the high life. She'd hitched her wagon to the stars and by gosh, she was on her way.

"Are you sure it's okay to borrow?" she directed at Zane.

"Of course, we couldn't pay for that kind of advertising. You must wear it with pride."

"I certainly will and I've got the perfect shoes to go with-"

"The red sparkly ones," Brendon interrupted. "Oh they'll be simply divine."

A sudden high-pitched ringing came from the changing room.

"That's my phone, hang on." Megan darted back into the cubicle and rummaged in her handbag. "Where are you?" She finally found it. Without glancing at the screen she answered it, fully expecting it to cut out as she'd left it so long.

"Hey, sexy English girl, how you doin'?"

"Tate?"

"Yeah, you sound flustered, what are you up to?"

"Er, just some business stuff. A meeting, you know."

"Ah yes, you're a high-powered business girl aren't you? Not just a gorgeous face."

"Well I…" She stared in the mirror and ran her free hand over her waist.

"I want to see you soon," he said. "Let's not wait until next week."

"Okay, what did you have in mind?"

"I'm going to be in Santa Monica all day tomorrow, filming. But it's bound to be slow, new director and everything. Why don't you swing by, whenever suits you, and we'll grab some lunch together?"

"That sounds nice."

"Yeah, it will be real nice. Real nice to see you." He lowered his voice. "I've been thinking about you a lot."

"Have you?"

"Yeah, we have a connection, don't we? I can feel it. You and me. Tate and Megan."

His words surprised her. They'd only had one interaction. Sure, she'd thought he was an Adonis in the looks department but she hadn't felt a real connection yet.

"I feel drawn to you," he went on, "which is why I had to call."

"Oh, well, thanks, you know, for calling."

"So you'll come on set tomorrow."

"Yes, I'm sure I'll find time. Brendon and I have some work to do but—"

Tate chuckled. "Bring Brendon, I'll introduce him to some of the life guards, he'll love it."

"Yes, you're not wrong there." Megan glanced at Brendon who had his head lowered with Zane's—they appeared to be studying paperwork. "We'll come by early afternoon then."

"Perfect."

The line went dead.

So that was it. Tate had called. They were seeing each other tomorrow, *on set*. How wonderfully LA that sounded.

"Who was that?" Brendon called.

"Oh, only Tate."

"Only Tate!" His voice had gone up an octave.

"Jeez, she's so ultra-cool about having Tate Simmons call her up." Zane rolled his eyes. "Seriously, that girl is born to be a star."

5

James

The sound of the breaking waves filtered into James' consciousness before he was even fully awake. It was one of the best things about being back in Los Angeles. His fashionably salt-beaten Malibu beach house was set against the sand and had endless views of the ocean that whispered to him day and night. Waking up to the Pacific ebbing its constant energy and strength was idyllic.

He stretched out his legs, the cotton sheet cool on his skin. Not so long ago he'd had Megan in his bed and life and had hoped that she might join him in LA. He'd imagined having her here with him in the mornings. She'd be enjoying the scent of the briny breeze and sipping freshly squeezed juice on his decking. He'd thought about her smile and seeing her in his home — in the lounge or on the hammock — waiting for him when he came back from a day's work. He'd been crazy enough to think of how he'd take her into his arms, kiss her, feel her embrace and let the tension of the day soak from him.

There'd also been restaurants he'd planned on taking her to. Movies he'd planned to enjoy with her in some of the city's iconic theatres. Hell, he'd even hoped for strolls along the pier at Santa Monica and had had childish daydreams of riding the Ferris wheel and eating candyfloss while holding her hand.

But none of that was to be.

He sighed and opened his eyes to the light. He could tell by the bleached sunshine splintering around the cracks in his blinds that yet another blistering hot day was to come.

Not that he minded. The London weather had got old

pretty quickly. He might have had to spend a fair bit of time in the studio the last month but he liked to feel the sun on his face and the heat of summer on his shoulders when he did emerge from the editing cave.

Still, if he could have had a future with Megan Rose Winter then perhaps he'd have tolerated the English drizzle and the clouds. She was warm and sunny and more than made up for inclement weather. He'd thought they'd started something special, that she'd felt the same. How had he got it so wrong? Okay so he didn't consider himself to be an expert when it came to the opposite sex, but he liked to think that he had the measure of people. It was what he did—he figured out the way humans ticked through his documentaries. And although Megan had been like a nervous filly at times, had blown hot one minute and cold the next, he thought he'd seen real passion and attraction in her eyes. In fact he was sure of it. They'd made love in a way that had connected their souls, not just their bodies.

He huffed at his error of judgement and bad luck as he got out of bed.

What was the point in thinking of Megan at the start and end of each day and a hundred times in between? Their fledgling relationship was history and she was thousands of miles away from him.

He flicked on the shower and stepped in, glad of the initial blast of cool water that woke him fully. He had things to do today—it was the first day of meeting the real-life stars of the *Baywatch*-style documentary he'd inherited. He needed to get to grips with how they were going to progress with the narrator and the scenes.

He reached for the shampoo and scrubbed at his hair. Damn Leon Walder for spending his days and nights getting to the bottom of the next bottle. James wasn't into fly-on-the-wall documentaries about *Baywatch* beauties— how would that contribute to the state of the world? His work was critically acclaimed for its in-depth analysis of difficult issues. He was the sort of director who took on the cases no one else wanted to. It was what his reputation was built on—being fearless, fighting for justice, taking the world of television documenting to the edge.

He had even been nominated for a Best Director Award.

He soaped up and rinsed. If he could be bothered to go to the ceremony, that was. He had a feeling that the project his boss Rue Skimmer had thrown at him was going to push him to the edge of his sanity.

And the narrator, the hot-shot A-lister who he'd been told to keep happy, he really didn't have time for him. He hadn't even known Tate Simmons was branching out from his usual big budget, big action movies. He was a pretty face, sure, but he couldn't understand the appeal.

He stepped out and dried. He guessed Tate's appeal was mainly to the females on the planet. With his blue eyes and blond hair, he was like countless other Hollywood beaus who'd graced the screens.

As he dragged on boxers then jeans, James hoped that Tate wouldn't be a diva. That was the last thing he had time for. What he wanted to do was get this goddamn project off his back, submit his next proposal to Rue and hopefully get a filming date scheduled into the calendar. He had some thoughts already and had done a fair bit of research. The drug cartels in Central America were getting out of hand and making many people's lives a misery. He wanted to highlight that to the world, show the big power nations what was going on and force them to acknowledge the problem. Just because it wasn't over their threshold didn't mean to say it wasn't on their doorstep.

James opted for loose cotton chinos and a red Tommy polo. He went for brown leather brogues since he'd be on the beach most of the day, and after running his fingers through his hair, he slipped on a pair of Calvin Klein sunglasses

After a power breakfast of a green smoothie and a bowl of granola, he headed out of the door. He was picking Grant up on his way in—carpooling was the best option when getting around LA as it meant they could use the near empty lanes on the freeway.

"Hey buddy, how you doing?" Grant said, hopping into James' BMW.

"Great, you?"

"Yep, just about back on Pacific time now, struggled to get out of bed this morning, though." Grant slammed the door and buckled up.

"Probably would have been easier if you hadn't had a hot date last night," James said, pulling back into the traffic.

Grant chuckled. "Yeah, that's true. She was worth it mind you."

"You seeing her again?"

"Yes, probably. Maybe. I'll see."

"Oh, you're such a commitment-phobe."

"No I'm not, I'm just picky." Grant shrugged. "Nothing wrong with that."

"So what's her name?"

"Tara, she's an actress."

"Isn't everyone in this town?" James clicked his tongue off the roof of his mouth.

"Yep, and if they're not in front of the camera they're behind it, like us. Gotta make a living somehow. Down that way..." Grant pointed. "There's parking near the pier for the crew apparently."

James went the way Grant had directed. "I'll be glad when this is over."

"Yeah, gonna feel like I've fallen out of the ugly tree all day having to work with Tate Simmons. Guys that look like him should be banished, they just make life harder for mere mortals like us."

"Look on the bright side, what he has in looks he's likely lacking in personality." James chuckled.

"Yeah, I heard he's a bit of an airhead, not the brightest

spark in the fire."

"See, no one has everything."

"Well he was going out with Titiana for a while, the lead singer of Black Rogue, she's seriously hot. I'd feel like I had everything if I had her."

"He's not seeing her anymore?"

"Nah, they split. Shame, she might have dropped by the set to see him."

James spotted the crew vans and a couple of security guys dressed in bright orange high viz vests at the end of the street. He made his way towards them.

When he reached the first security guy, he rolled down his window.

"Hey there," the guy said.

"Hi, James Carter, director. Can we park over there?" James nodded at a free space.

"Ah yes, of course, sir, that will be just great." He stepped back and waved them in.

"Sir," Grant said as the window closed. "Wow, you are going up in the world."

"Won't last." James manoeuvred into the parking spot. "Not when they realise I'm not messing about here. I want to get this done and dusted and hot foot away from this crap Walder left me to clear up—the sooner the better."

"Which means you'll be full steam ahead, no slacking, no slinking off early and no long, lazy lunches."

"Exactly. It's nose to the grindstone. I want this wrapped up." He turned the engine off. "ASAP."

They both climbed out and headed towards the largest trailer, their feet sinking in the shingle ground.

"You got our next project submitted yet?"

"No, I still need to get the proposal together." James paused and rested his hand on Grant's shoulder. "Are you sure you're in? It's going to be a risky one."

Grant huffed. "I'm your right-hand man, where the hell would you be if things got risky and I wasn't there?"

James smiled. He wouldn't, probably couldn't, head to

Central America without Grant at his side. He might be up for a laugh, enjoy his time with the ladies and having a beer and a shout at the baseball, but when push came to shove he could be relied upon. Grant was good in a crisis, he had a level head and was a fast thinker, and he also had a knack for getting brilliant shots when everyone else was running for cover.

"Thanks, mate." James smiled. "But you know I have to ask."

"You don't. I'm there for you. What we do is special."

"It will be interesting to see if *Poor Choices* gets credited by the panel at next week's ceremony."

"They'd be crazy not to. Rue did a good job getting it subbed on deadline day, it's not even been aired yet."

"Yes, he's not all bad. Come on, let's go meet the crew."

An hour later, James and Grant were on the beach. Grant was heading up a small team of camera, lighting and sound guys, and James was going through the day's schedule with the lifeguards who'd agreed to be part of the fly-on-the-wall. They didn't look exactly like the *Baywatch* stars — some were older, some not as fit — but there were several beauties who could have graced the cover of a magazine or shot to fame on the cult TV show.

"So we have quite a few interviews already in the bank that Walder did before he…got sick. And I'd like to expand on those. Rhet…" James nodded at the most senior lifeguard. "If you could give us a demonstration of rescuing from about two hundred yards out then we can have Tate introduce the situation."

"We just gonna wait till someone starts to drown?" Rhet asked with a huff.

"No, not at all. We haven't got time to wait for that, though it would be good if it did happen." James paused. He hoped that hadn't sounded callous. "I'm sorry. What

I mean is it would be more authentic. Naturally we don't want anyone to get into difficulties out there." He nodded at the deep blue rollers that were cresting and crashing just yards from them. "What we need is a volunteer to look like they're in trouble. One of you, preferably."

"I don't mind doing it?" A pretty young lifeguard with wavy red hair pulled into a high ponytail smiled at James. "You want me to go and get changed out of this red suit?" She pulled at the shoulder strap and swiped her tongue over her bottom lip.

"I, er…yes. That way you won't look like a member of the team."

"But I'll be fine if Rhet can't save me." She stood and after flicking her hair, dashed off to the lifeguard hut.

"Huh, as if," Rhet said, standing. "So where is Tate? He's usually late but today he's pushing it." He glanced at his chunky black watch.

James looked around and frowned. He needed his narrator to be on shot. Without him this was all pointless.

"There he is," Grant said, pointing into the distance.

Sure enough, James could see a tall blond superstar actor heading their way. He had a small entourage with him—a couple of burly security guys from the trailer and behind them several fans. The security at the edge of the set opened up the cordon and Tate turned and gave the fans a smile and a wave.

"Good," James said, studying his notes. "That means we can get this show on the road."

"Hey, folks, sorry about the delay, you know how it is," Tate said, strutting up to James and casting a glance over the rest of the crew. "You must be the new director."

"Yes, James Carter. Pleased to meet you."

"Yeah, likewise. Hope you don't like the liquor as much as the last one." Tate slapped James on the shoulder. "Spent most of his time sneaking back to the trailer for a few slugs of Jack D."

"I think we can safely say Jack D and I are not on regular

meeting terms. Now I'd really like to get this going, it's gone noon."

"*Gone noon.* Awesome, you have such a neat Brit accent, just what I need to be around. My next movie I'm playing a lord, so I need all the practice I can get." Tate had spoken with an upper class English accent.

"Sounds like you're doing fine," James said, forcing a smile. "If I can just fill you in on what we're about to do here and what your lines are today, that would be great."

"Sure, buddy, go ahead." Again, Tate slapped James on the shoulder.

James gritted his teeth. This was going to be worse than he'd thought.

Soon they had the camera rolling. Grant had filming and sound under control, James had the co-ordination going to plan and the lifeguards acted like pros. All Tate had had to do was introduce the sequence then add live commentary. He performed to a standard James could cope with, though he still couldn't understand why the studio had picked him for this project.

Oh yeah, because he looks the part. That's why.

The rescue sequence was soon in the bag. "Great, people, thank you. We'll take..." James checked the time on his phone. "Half an hour for refreshments then we've got one more thing I want to get nailed before sundown."

"Thirty minutes?" Tate said, shaking his head. "That'll hardly get me to a restaurant and seated, let alone served and time to eat."

"Sorry, buddy." James feigned a pained expression. "Guess you'll just have to eat in the trailer like us common folk."

Tate frowned. "Walder let us have longer and I presumed you would too, so I've made arrangements."

He shielded his eyes from the sun and glanced up and down the beach.

A small crowd had gathered behind the cordon to watch the activity of the crew and Tate.

"So unarrange them," James said sharply. "Sorry, but this is a working day and that's what we're doing, working."

"Well I know that, but... Oh wait, here she is..." He pointed over James' shoulder.

"Who?" James said, turning.

"My date. Sorry, I'll be as quick as I can." He raised his hand. "Hey, security let that one through, and her buddy."

James watched the crowd part slightly as the rope was released to allow a man and a woman to walk onto their section of the beach.

He suddenly felt as though his feet were sinking into the sand deep, deep, deeper. His head spun and he blinked several times. He plucked his shades off and held them by the tip of the arm.

It couldn't be. His mind was playing a trick on him. He'd been so desperate to see her his brain cells had conjured her image to stand right in front of him. Not only that, but to stand in front of him as someone this jerk, Tate, was expecting.

Megan.

It couldn't be.

He pressed his fingers to the bridge of his nose and squeezed, glanced at his feet. When he looked back up would she still be there?

No. This is impossible.

He looked back up. She was still as real as the sand and the waves. Her hair was piled high and a few tendrils caught on the breeze wafting around her cheeks. She wore her usual sexy red lipstick and a long black beach dress dotted with tiny white flowers. On her wrist was a collection of silver bangles.

His heart lurched. She was beautiful. In this city constantly striving for perfection, she knocked them all off the shelf. She *was* perfect, and not only that, she was effortlessly perfect. It was the way she held herself, the tilt of her chin, the slope of her delicately tanned shoulders and how the dress dipped in at her waist then flared over her hips.

"What's she doing here?" he heard himself mutter.

"She's my new girl," Tate said. "And I'm taking her for lunch. We'll be as quick as we can, but hey, would you rush a date with a hot chick like that?" He chuckled.

James felt as though all the veins in his body had suddenly become too tight to house his blood. His temples pounded and his throat constricted.

Megan swept her gaze around the gaggle of crew and lifeguards. She saw Tate and raised her hand with a smile. But the smile never went to its usual gorgeous full beam. Instead it froze halfway there and her arm dropped to her side.

She stared at James and came to a halt several feet from where he stood with Tate.

"Bloody hell," Grant muttered at James' side. "Isn't that...?"

"Megan," Tate said, walking up to her and reaching for her hand. He drew it to his mouth and kissed her knuckles. A series of clicks went off in the crowd, iPhones going crazy for photographs.

Megan didn't take her attention from James. Her mouth hung slack and a slight crease had formed between her eyes.

James quickly put his shades back on.

Megan is with Tate? How the hell has that happened? And when?

Not long ago he'd been with her. Then he'd seen that chap in her apartment — which he hadn't managed to get to the bottom of — and now Tate was taking her to lunch.

Tate bloody Simmons.

Of all the men in the world!

"Megan, meet my new boss, James Carter, he's turning out to be a real slave driver." Tate pulled Megan across the sand to stand before James. "I'm afraid we won't be able to have a long, lazy liquid lunch." He winked at her. "Not today anyway."

"James," Megan said, her face a little paler now than

when he'd first seen her.

"Why are you…here?" James managed.

"I invited her," Tate said, squaring his shoulders.

"Why are *you* here?" Megan said, pulling her hand from Tate's and folding her arms. Her mouth was a thin, straight line and she swallowed quickly.

"I'm working," James said.

"Working?" She looked confused.

"Yes. I'm a director remember, and I'm directing this goddamn programme because the pisshead who was supposed to be doing it has gone on a bender and left me to clear up the crap."

"Oh."

She looked hurt by his sharp words and instantly James felt bad. What he really wanted to do was wrap her in his arms and whisper in her ear that they should give it another try. Remind her that they'd been so good together, that something great had been about to happen for both of them.

Till she'd thrown it all away by doing her usual trick of running.

Well, this time he'd found where she'd run to. She'd run the wrong way, or rather the right way, towards him.

"Do you guys er…know each other?" Tate asked, looking between them.

"You could say that." Grant sniggered then looked at James.

James frowned and pursed his lips. He mimicked Megan's stance and folded his arms.

"Sorry, mate," Grant said with a shrug. He turned back to a piece of filming equipment and started fiddling.

"Yes," Megan said quietly. "We do know each other."

6

Megan

Megan's world was spinning. The man she'd been dreaming about was standing in front of her looking as dark and devastatingly gorgeous as he always had.

The sun was right behind him, almost like a halo, and all she wanted to do was lean into his arms, snuggle against his neck and remind herself of the feel of his skin and the scent of his hair.

But of course she couldn't. She was *with* Tate.

What kind of crazy collision of the stars had occurred to make this happen? Had some butterfly flapped its wings the wrong way in Australia and now this was the devastation in LA?

The thought of Australia pulled at her heartstrings. What she wouldn't do to have her mum and her sister with her right now. She could use the support of family.

"You okay, sweetpea?" Brendon rested his hand on her arm.

"Yes...just..." *Surprised. Shocked. Elated. Devastated.* A pile of emotions tumbled through her like boulders toppling down a mountainside.

"Oh, so how do you know each other?" Tate asked, raising his perfectly neat eyebrows. "Ah, no don't tell me, you're both British right, you know each other from home."

"It's a big place." Brendon rubbed his hands together. "They know each other because —"

"We just do," James said sharply. He threw Brendon a warning look.

Megan sucked in a quick breath, her chest hitching against her dress. James didn't even want to label what they'd had. It must have been a flash in the pan to him, not worth mentioning or even remembering. She was a girl who'd been and gone like a ship passing in the night.

Well she'd show him. He hadn't given her a chance to explain about Dylan or even had the courtesy to answer her texts and calls. And now this. Acting like she was nothing to him when only a short time ago he'd been dragging her into cupboards at Grace Studios, kissing her senseless and telling her all the sexy things he'd wanted to do to her.

Tate reached for her hand and twined his fingers with hers. Megan allowed him to and straightened her back. If James had moved on, she'd just have to show him that she had too and who better to move on with than a Hollywood hottie.

"Well, this is all very nice and all, this catching up thing," Tate said. "But we're on an enforced time limit here so we should go and eat before we drop down dead with hunger." He nodded at Brendon. "You spare wheeling or you hanging out at the beach?"

"I'll hang out here." Brendon cast an appreciative glance over the lifeguards who were gathering to head off to lunch. "I'll see you later."

"Are you sure, Brendon?" Megan asked.

"Yes, yes, you kids go and have fun." He looked between Tate and James, clearly wondering if he'd spark another reaction from James.

Megan bit on her bottom lip and frowned at Brendon. She knew he was loving the drama of the moment. It was all right for him, she thought, her world was imploding and his was lighting up with the spectacle of her caught in a love triangle — again.

"I know this neat little sushi place, just off the beach. We'll go fill up on sashimi, shall we?" Tate said, tugging her hand.

"That sounds nice." Megan wasn't sure what sashimi was but she'd give it a go. Not that she had much appetite. Right now her stomach was roiling and a bite of bile was nipping at her gullet.

She cast one more look at James.

He'd turned away from her. His broad back was slightly hunched and his hands were shoved deep into the pockets of his trousers. His attention was set firmly on the ocean and the surfers who were rolling in.

Her eyes stung a little and she blinked to control any tears that might try to make themselves known. It seemed he couldn't even stand to look at her.

Tate tugged her hand then led her away from the set. Each time her feet sank into the sand, her heart sank a little more too. How quickly she'd gone from being lighthearted and moving on with her life to being soul-achingly desperate to turn back the clock. What she wouldn't do to have James leading her towards the pier and taking her for lunch. She longed to have him smile at her the way Tate just had, kiss her hand, tell her about a neat little place they could spend some time in each other's company.

She could smell Tate's aftershave. It was heady and expensive and undeniably nice but it wasn't James' rich scent, the delicious flavours that made her think of his smile, his embrace and the way he held her close.

"We'll head to the trailer and shake this crowd," Tate said, nodding at a growing group of young fans. "Then we'll slip out the back to the restaurant, should be okay. It's only a block away."

"Whatever you think is best," Megan managed. Should she still go to lunch with Tate? Perhaps she should call the whole thing off? Lunch, the award ceremony, them being a thing? She didn't mind a bit of publicity and it was all good for Winter Shoes but she knew the photographs the crowd had taken of her and Tate on the beach would soon be all over social media.

Was she ready for that?

She was feeling fragile enough as it was without being thrust into the spotlight. Not just any spotlight, but the red-carpet, Hollywood spotlight. It didn't get any brighter than that.

Yet she and Brendon had talked about this the evening before. It was all amazing publicity for the business, in fact Tate couldn't be better publicity. Being romantically linked to him was like a fast train to success.

Tate pressed his hand into the small of her back and urged her walk a little quicker. A couple of security men flanked them and several fans rallied close.

"Autograph this, Tate."

"Just one picture."

"Who is your girlfriend?"

"Can you sign this for me?"

"What's your name, girl?"

"Later," he said, ducking his head and putting a hand in the air. "All of it later. I'm short on time right now."

"Tate. Tate."

The voices faded as Megan stepped into the trailer.

Tate was close behind her.

He shut the door and blew out a breath.

"Do you ever get used to that?" she asked, brushing out a crease in her dress.

"What, being hassled?"

"No, not that, I mean having people follow you?" She wasn't sure it was something she'd want to live with. "Asking for stuff."

"Yeah, I guess. So it was super-nice the other day when you didn't want anything from me and didn't recognise me. It made me feel normal for a change. Haven't had that feeling in a while." He stepped up close and stroked the back of his index finger down her cheek. "And I should also say thanks for turning up today. Not easy to be flung into the crowds this way."

"I said I would." Once again she stared into his bluer than blue eyes. She could see why he lit up a big screen and made audiences swoon when he turned them to the camera lens.

"People don't always do what they say they're going to do," Tate said in a low voice. "But I do."

Megan could feel her heart tripping along. The trailer was hot and smelled of coffee. It was also dark and full of shadows after the dazzling light outside.

"Maybe we should skip lunch," Tate said, lowering his head. "And get better acquainted before the ceremony next week."

He swept his lips over Megan's. She gasped a little and reached out to hold onto his forearms.

He smiled down at her. "You taste of sunshine. A ray of beautiful English sunshine." He dipped his head again and pressed a harder kiss over her mouth. As he did so, he wound one hand around her waist and curled his other around the nape of her neck. He pulled her against the length of his body.

"Tate!" She pulled back. "Please...I..."

"What's the problem?" He swiped his tongue over his bottom lip as though gathering her flavour.

She stared up at him.

"Are you wondering if the trailer has a bedroom?" He raised his eyebrows. "Because it does, a very comfortable one."

"No, it's not that." She pushed away from him.

He dropped his hands to his sides.

Megan glanced at the window at the end of the living area. It had thin black blinds that were nearly closed yet she could still make out the beach and a few of the film crew hanging around. Was James one of them? Had he seen her come into this trailer? Was he right this minute thinking she was getting frisky with Tate Simmons?

Her guts wrenched and a tightening in her chest made her press her fist over her sternum.

"Megan?" Tate said, his expression now one of concern. "Are you okay?"

"Yes...I mean no. It's too hot in here. Can we go?"

"Yes, of course. This way." He studied her for a second then turned. "There's another exit out the back. It leads to an alley and from there we can go where we want." He grabbed a cap and a pair of sunglasses and put them on. "Let's do this." He grinned.

Megan followed him past the kitchen area and into what looked like a storeroom for spare filming equipment. Sure enough, there was another exit.

Tate opened it and held out his hand. "Come on, this way."

She took his hand and stepped down to the gravel. She wished that James had seen her leave. That he didn't think she was still in the trailer with Tate. Maybe she should text Brendon?

"It's through here," Tate said.

"Have you done this before?"

"What, pretended to be one place when I'm somewhere else so I can have lunch in peace with a pretty girl?" He flashed her a grin. "No, never."

She didn't believe him for a moment, but she didn't want to argue. "I just have to send a text."

"Sure. Go ahead."

As they walked down a quiet backstreet she quickly tapped out a message to Brendon.

OMG! Can you believe J is HERE! If u saw me go in trailer we not there now. Secret back door. Off to restaurant please tell J that if you can so he doesn't think...you know... XOXO

She hit send and hoped that Brendon would be able to read between the lines and in turn read her fears and emotions. She had every faith in him. He knew her better than anyone, well except perhaps for Georgie.

Oh, Georgie. I wish you were here now to tell me what to do.

"This is it," Tate said, pushing into a small Japanese restaurant.

"That was quick."

"Yeah, I said it wasn't far." He ushered Megan in.

The small dining area was elegant and decorated entirely in white. Several dark beams on the ceiling and walls were the only things that broke up the starkness. The tables were dressed in white linen, and white vases on the tables held white orchids. Pictures of white blossom trees hung on the walls and the floor was polished white tiles.

"Good afternoon, sir, madam," said a waitress also dressed in white. "Table for two?" A hint of recognition flashed over her eyes as she looked at Tate but she remained professional.

"Yes," Tate said. "Away from the door and window, you have a booth, at the back?"

"Certainly, sir. This way."

Megan followed Tate past several diners, some of whom gave Tate a second glance.

Quickly they were settled in a white leather booth that screened them from other diners and passers-by.

"Here is specials for today." The Japanese waitress held out two menus.

"We'll just have a chef selection," Tate said. "We're a bit short on time." He looked at Megan. "That's okay, isn't it?"

"Er, yes, sure." She knotted her fingers in her lap. That was the kind of thing her ex Dylan would have said. He had always ordered for her, made decisions for her, chosen what they'd do, where they'd go. Being free from Dylan was one of the things that had put a spring in her step over the summer.

"Yes, sir." The waitress disappeared—she seemed to glide rather than walk, and held her hands in front of her, tightly clasped.

"I was hoping we'd have longer." Tate put his elbows on the table and tapped his fingers together. "But this new director, James, he's got a whip on our butts."

"I thought you only started working with James Carter today." Just saying his name sent a rush of heat through her body. She wanted to say *my* James, that Tate had only just started working with *her* James today—but of course she didn't.

"Yeah, we did. I was a bit late, got caught up at the gym, I think that annoyed him a bit." He smiled. "But I gotta keep in shape, can't take my eye off the ball when it comes to keeping my body in top-rate condition."

"No, of course not." And she was sure his army of fans would agree that he did a fine job of staying in shape.

"It would cost me lead parts you know, if I let myself go, and I need them. I gotta keep on rolling out the movies, getting those bucks in the bank and making my name."

"I'd say you've already done that."

"Well yeah, here in the US, but clearly world domination hasn't kicked in. You Brits didn't know me the other day."

"I don't go to the cinema very often. I'm busy with Winter Shoes and all that. I'm sure I would have recognised you if I did go more. My friend, Georgie, she'd heard of you."

"Ahh..." He cocked his head and smirked. "So you've been talking about me to your buddy. I guess I should take that as a good sign."

"Well, yes, I mean it's very exciting, the award ceremony and everything. I can't wait." Damn, should she still go with him? What about James? It would likely mean even more pictures of her and Tate together. She felt in such a dither about what to do.

James hates me. He couldn't even look at me.

"Yeah, it is real exciting." Tate sat back as a jug of water packed with ice, lemon and limes was set before them. "And hopefully I can get your designs some exposure too."

"Well that's not the reason I'm going with you."

"Of course not, but don't feel bad about that if some exposure happens, I'm happy to help."

"Are you sure, because —?"

"Don't sweat it." He picked up his drink. "You're very talented, I'd bet my last buck on it. You just need a break and if that's me, well, all the better." He paused. "Maybe I'll be lucky enough to get another kiss as a way of thanks."

Megan looked at his sensual mouth. Kissing Tate Simmons wasn't the worst thing in the world to do and many women dreamed of it but equally she didn't want to feel like she'd used him or that there'd been a deal. Because there was no way she was going to jump into bed with him, even if millions would think she needed her head testing for feeling that way. It just wasn't the sort of girl she was.

"Here, for you. Chef hopes very much you enjoy." The waitress set a large sharing platter between them. It was set with slivers of pink salmon. Rolls of rice were topped with a host of interesting looking morsels.

"I could live on this," Tate said. "Well, this and protein drinks. I gotta have them, keep the muscle tone. But this, the fish it's good for hair and nails and stuff."

Megan popped in a small piece of sushi and watched Tate do the same. He was talking about his hair and nails? She'd never been with a guy who thought of that kind of stuff — not counting Brendon, but that was different.

"Do you like it?" Tate asked.

"Yes, it's lovely." She paused and took a sip of water. "So why is James being such a whip wielder?"

"Oh he's a big ass director who really doesn't want to be doing this TV thing. Apparently it's not his *style*." Tate did finger quotes around the last word. "But you must be aware of that right, if you know him?"

"Well, I think he is into more serious, exposure type stuff."

"Saving the planet, eco-warrior, tree hugging?"

"No, more like showing reality to people who are comfy at home living in their own bubble. Exposing poverty and war and injustice, that kind of thing."

Tate raised his eyebrows. "Sounds very commendable." He paused. "How do you know him again?"

Megan looked away and pretended to study the food platter between them.

"Megan?"

"We worked near each other in London."

"Ah, I see…"

"Yes, we bumped into each other a few times. Had the odd drink, you know."

Tate raised his eyebrows and held a piece of sushi halfway

between the platter and his mouth. "You dated him? You and hot-shot director were…?"

Megan pursed her lips. Did she want to answer that question? James had to work with Tate. Would Tate gloat about the fact that he had James' girl? Tate was supposed to be doing what James told him to do but would this give him leverage to mock?

But she'd never been James' girl. Not really. They'd had a few dates and spent the night together. The fact that it had been one of the most intense, sexy, deeply emotional nights of her life had nothing to do with it.

She'd messed up by running at the first bit of trouble between them and had ruined it all.

"Whoa, you don't need to tell me anything," Tate said, grinning. "I can see it in your face. You two were an item."

A wave of panic went through her. "Well, not really. I mean there was maybe a spark…"

"A spark or an inferno?" Tate waggled his eyebrows.

None of your damn business.

Megan reached for her water, her hand a little shaky. She took a gulp then set it down. The coolness flooding her body dampened her rising temper.

"It was nothing," she said. "Nothing at all. It was just a surprise to see each other today."

"You didn't know he was here in LA?"

"No. We haven't been in touch for a while." She picked up another piece of sushi and ate it.

Tate did the same. When he'd swallowed he shrugged. "Let's not talk about *him* anyway, let's talk about what sights you've still got to see in LA. And how is the house? You had your first night there, didn't you?"

"Yes." Megan relaxed a little, pleased to have the conversation moving on from James. "It was very comfortable and quiet and Dirk is a total sweetheart."

Tate laughed. "Don't be fooled, he's a rich boy with a penchant for the white stuff. But he's cool, he'll be having the time of his life mooching around Malaysia. You enjoy his place while you're here. He'll be glad to have it occupied, keeps it more secure."

"Yes, we will. It's lovely."

"So how is the shoe world going?"

"Oh, exciting actually. The shop on Rodeo Drive that's giving me shelf space is holding a launch party for me. I'm so excited."

"That sounds awesome." He paused. "They do that, for shoes?"

"Yes, of course."

"Guess I never really thought about it."

Megan pressed her lips together. She was beyond excited about the launch, it sounded like Brendon and Zane had it all worked out and it was going to be amazing. It would make up for this mess she'd found herself in, well some of the way.

"So do you have a dress for the ceremony?" Tate asked, before popping the last bit of food from the platter into his mouth.

"Yes, a red one, it's long."

"Very nice. I'll be in Armani. Got a new deal coming up with them, but don't say anything." He winked. "All I will say is there's going to be some very *brief* photographs for my fans to enjoy. Maybe I could send a signed one to your friend in England who *has* heard of me."

"Georgie," Megan said. She shook her head and grinned. "I'm sure she'd love it." *But not as much as you love you.* But she didn't say that, she took another mouthful of cool water and held the words in. He was all about him but his heart seemed to be in the right place.

7

"I cannot believe you're not ready," Brendon shouted from the front door of their new home. "This is your big day, birthday girl."

"I am, I really am..." Megan puffed as she scooped up lipstick, powder and her phone and shoved them in her new Fendi purse. "Is Gucci ready?"

"Of course he is and he looks sensational in his new Prada outfit, don't you, Gucci-Gucci-coo."

There'd been an hour-long debate in Posh Paws the day before about what best to put Gucci in. It was too cliché for him to wear Gucci apparently, and the sparkly black leather jacket from Louis Vuitton just wasn't him. In the end, a gold waistcoat had won the contest because it had a matching top hat complete with tiny earholes.

Megan checked her makeup for the last time then slipped into her favourite design of last season. A thirty millimetre, diamanté studded pair of the palest blue heels imaginable, they had peep toes and she'd found the perfect matching shade to paint her toenails.

She'd teamed it with a fitted dress — again the same pale blue — that although short and showed off her now tanned legs had a high collar and managed to look demure. With her hair professionally pinned up and long silver earrings in that almost touched her shoulders, she felt ready for the official launch of Winter Shoes onto Rodeo Drive.

Hurriedly, she dashed across the bedroom, managing to create a bluster of air movement that knocked down her two birthday cards. She paused and bent to retrieve them. The larger of the pair was from her parents. It was tall and slim and had pictures of shoes floating on clouds on it. She set it back on her cabinet. The other was from Georgie and had a cute picture of two little girls holding hands and jumping into a muddy puddle in wellington boots. Above the image were the words, *Friends who jump in puddles together jump through life together.*

Megan pressed a quick kiss to the card and set it by the other one. This would be the first birthday she could remember since her and Georgie had met that they wouldn't be spending together. It was hard. As if there was a light in her day that just wasn't shining.

"Megan Rose Winter, I swear I will go to *your* party without you in a minute."

"I'm there now." Megan pulled in a deep breath, before heading out of the bedroom and down the stairs.

Brendon stood in the hallway looking very dapper in tight blood-red jeans and a white silk shirt. He'd added a cravat in the same red, and his crocodile-leather, wickedly pointed shoes were scarlet and so highly polished it was almost possible for Gucci to study his little reflection in them.

"Oh my, you do indeed look like a woman who should be dating a Hollywood superstar." He clasped his hands beneath his chin. "Oh, wait. You are!" He chuckled and bent to scoop up Gucci. "Come on, there is a cab waiting for us."

Megan locked up the door and headed down the small path after Brendon. Her heels made sharp clicking noises and her dress was tight around her thighs. She felt good, no, more than good. This was a pretty amazing way to be spending her thirtieth birthday. A party, a new city, a new future, a new man…

A new man.

But she still liked the old one…

No, she couldn't think that way. Well, not today anyway. Today she would put on her best professional smile, woo the customers and clients Zane and Brendon had invited to the launch and enjoy living the high life.

They rode the short cab trip up into Beverley Hills and

alighted directly outside LA Hype. Brendon paid the fare as Megan stared at the huge bunch of balloons that hung from a rail above the shop window.

She guessed there were over one hundred and each colour exactly matched one of the shoes she was showcasing today. They were also sparkly and had white ribbons hanging from them. They dominated the shop and made it stand out from all the others on Rodeo Drive.

A red carpet with black ropes sectioning it off edged into the walkway, and a sign on a black stand read *Launch of Winter Shoes, invitation only.*

"Really, invitation only?" Megan asked. "Don't we want customers?"

"Well yes, of course," Brendon said, "but not today, and in this town of excess the most sought after thing is exclusivity. Make Winter Shoes available to everyone from the word go and it's too easy. Make them available for the select few, and the masses, well the masses with cash, will come flocking."

"Oh, okay."

"But don't worry, there's plenty of people on the guest list. Zane's boutique will be full of Winter Shoes admirers before we know it and some of them you may have even seen before." He winked.

"What do you mean?"

"Sweetpea, believe it or not, Zane has some celebrities in that little black book of his that are all looking to dress to impress." He nodded seriously.

"Mmm, I see." For a moment Megan had wondered if maybe her family had made the trip to surprise her, if that's what Brendon had meant when he'd said some of the people she'd seen before. After all, Sydney to LA wasn't an exhausting distance. Not like it had been to the UK. But it was silly to even think that. She'd seen them only last month and they'd been in such a frantic tizz of activity to get the party all organised that Brendon would never have had time to organise even an email to her parents and sister.

Brendon stepped up to the window. "What do you think of this?" He spread out his fingers as if offering the display to her.

"It's a piece of art." Megan's stomach did a roll of excitement and she placed her palms on the glass. This was really it. Her designs, her creations, her babies had made it. In pairs, they were set on ten sparkling towers, each one a different height. At the base of the display a pool of water glittered under spotlights and real silvery fish swam around the bottom of the pillars. Winter Shoes appeared to have risen from the ocean, been born like Venus. In fact the backdrop, as planned, was a copy of Botticelli's masterpiece of the beautiful goddess emerging from an oyster and several large shells were neatly placed around.

"It is exactly that, a masterpiece." Brendon pointed at the fish. "But Zane is a creative talent in his own right. To think of this, fish, Venus, the shells. So clever." He sighed.

"I agree…" She paused.

"What?"

"The fish won't get too hot will they?"

"Ahh…" Brendon tapped his nose. "He even thought of that. These little babies are tropical and he's got an alarmed thermometer to make sure they're perfectly happy during their stay here."

"Good."

"But come on, come on, don't worry about the fish. We need to get out of this heat ourselves before my hair flops and your nose gets shiny." He half-walked, half-skipped along the red carpet, Gucci's head bobbing with his actions.

Megan followed him into the coolness of the shop.

"Wow." She stopped in her tracks and looked around. The ceiling was a mass of yet more balloons — there were so many of them she couldn't see the roof at all.

"Ah, you're here…" Zane appeared. He wore a tuxedo and looked very handsome.

Brendon obviously thought so too. "Oh, look at you." He wolf-whistled. "You do scrub up well, Zane."

"Did you ever doubt it?" Zane put his hands on hips and jutted them to the left.

"This is incredible." Megan turned in a circle, taking it all in.

In the centre of the shop a huge round table was draped in silvery linen. More glittering towers, the tallest in the middle, held the rest of her collection and shells had been set out around their bases.

Two waitresses in smart black suits stood by a black counter that held champagne in flutes. A platter of caviar canapés sat on ice and a mountain of strawberries were piled into a crystal bowl.

"Lucile and Renee are serving, all you need to do is enjoy." Zane took Megan's hands in his. His skin was soft and his fingers delicate. "And of course schmooze with the guests."

"Thank you," Megan said, "I really mean it, thank you for this opportunity."

"This is only the start," he said. "Opportunities will be walking through that door all afternoon. We just need to harness them. Make them ours. Make them Winter Shoes."

Megan smiled. "It smells gorgeous in here, what is it?"

"Ah" — his eyes widened — "I'm glad you asked. It's actually bang on theme. It's a new perfume from Ruby Marlowe, one of our regular clients of course, called Venus, would you believe, so I've had a good spray around and added it into the timed fresheners."

"What a fabulous idea," Brendon said. "Only you could think of that."

"Well, yes, probably." Zane nodded modestly and let go of Megan's hands. He looked over at the waitresses. "Glass of bubbles for the birthday girl please, chop, chop. Anyone that comes in, as long as they're ticketed of course, must have champers immediately." He looked at Megan. "Now wait there."

Megan took the offered glass of champagne. "What's he doing?"

Brendon shrugged and also took a drink.

"Here," Zane said rushing back to them. "I have this for you, Megan." He handed her a photograph of Amanda Rush, a young actress she'd seen in a rom-com movie the month before. "Consider it a birthday present."

"I don't understand?"

Zane hopped from one foot to the other. "It's rumoured that Amanda Rush will be nominated for a Golden Globe."

"I'm not surprised, she's awesome." Megan was still confused. What did Amanda Rush have to do with her?

"And…"

"Oh do tell." Brendon put Gucci down and held up his hands. "We're dying here."

"And who do you think is styling her?" Zane rubbed his hands together.

"Er, you?" Megan guessed.

"Yes, yes, me, *moi*! And she was in here yesterday and chose, now this is of course confidential, strictly privileged information…" He looked sternly at them.

"Yes, naturally. Cross our hearts." Brendon swiped his fingers over his chest.

"Well, she's chosen one of *our* designs, a flowing Chantilly lace that is simply divine on her. It has accents of shell-pink around the bodice and when she spotted your new collection awaiting unveiling, she fell in love with these babies." He whizzed to the selection of Winter Shoes and plucked out a pale pink heel that had a lace overlay covering the fabric.

"She liked them?" Megan said, a slow smile spreading on her face.

"*Loved* them. Was almost kissing them. She's earmarked the dress and the shoes for the event. I can't imagine for a moment she'll change her mind."

"That's great." Megan took a sip of her drink. The bubbles popping on her tongue matched the thrilling giddy sensation in her stomach.

"And you know what they're like with the Golden Globes," Brendon said. "The so-called fashion gurus pick all the actors to bits, go over their choices of dress, shoes, purses in fine detail for weeks after the event. Everyone will have heard of Winter Shoes by the time the Oscars come around."

"And our lovely Ms Rush is their sweetheart. She never and I mean *never* ever gets it wrong." He cupped his hand around his mouth as though sharing a confidence with Megan and Brendon. "Partly because of me, I might add. I've been doing her for a year now." He laughed. "Well obviously not *doing* her that's not my style."

Brendon laughed too, then, "Yes, she's always top of the list of best dressed and there's usually pages dedicated to how to match her look."

"I know!" Zane beamed. "It's great for LA Hype and great for Winter Shoes. Of course it's not for a few months yet but that's fine, we have our finger in more pies than that." He raised his eyebrows and looked at the door. "Oh, and I think one is here now."

The door opened and three people entered the shop. Two men and a woman.

"Greta, darling, how are you?" Zane rushed up to the tall, slim female that Megan recognised as an actress on a sitcom that was aired in the UK called *Waiting on Life*.

"Zane, you look fabulous."

They both air-kissed with lots of *mwah* sounds going on.

A waitress glided forward and offered drinks to the new arrivals. The bigger of the two men, dressed entirely in black and wearing shades, shook his head and stayed standing by the door. Megan guessed he was Greta Breen's security.

"Yes, you may have one," Greta said to the red-haired man at her side.

He gave a small, almost grateful nod and took a drink.

Greta turned from him and looked expectantly at Zane.

"So this is Megan Winter, the hot new designer I was telling you about," Zane said, cupping Greta's elbow and leading her over to Megan and Brendon. The man with her, now sipping champagne, came too but kept his attention lowered.

"Nice to meet you," Megan said, holding out her hand.

"And you too. I'm all about the shoes." Greta took Megan's hand and shook. "And British designers, I can't resist. You get it, I mean the last Wang's I bought I couldn't wear, crushed my toes, so I went for Blahnik's for the Oscars, the balls of my feet were on fire and it showed in all the pap shots." She shook her head and took a sip of drink. "But I had some Jimmy Choos for Cannes and they were like wearing clouds despite being three inches high." She smiled and glanced at the display of Winter Shoes. "Zane assures me your collection is wonderfully comfortable and even better than Jimmy Choo."

"Oh yes." Megan reached for a modest height stiletto in lilac. "I insist on cushioning on the inner soles and with extra on the balls of the feet for all of my heels over ten millimetres, otherwise, as you say, it hurts, all the body weight forced onto one pressure point." She handed the shoe to Greta. "Feel it."

Greta passed her drink to the man at her side who still hadn't said a word.

"Mmm..." She poked at the heel. "I like it. Oh, and it's all glittery on the sole, very pretty." She smiled and studied Megan. "What size is this one?"

"Thirty-eight," Zane said quickly. "Your size, Greta, and might I just add, those in particular would go like strawberries and champagne with that lilac trouser suit you bought from here last week."

"Oh yes, you're right they would." She walked to a plush chair covered in dove grey fabric and sat. After toeing off a Louboutin mule she slipped her small foot into the shoe.

"Here's the other one." Zane was at her side.

"Thank you." She popped that one on her foot and stood. She was wearing a knee-length pencil skirt in a pale mushroom shade and the tones complemented each other in an unusual way.

"Oh they do feel nice," she said, nodding at Megan. "Very

nice."

"Try them out," Zane said, sweeping his hand in front of her.

Greta began to strut around the shop, her slim hips rolling and her head held high.

"I love her so much," Brendon whispered to Megan. He fanned his face. "I feel a little star-struck."

Megan grinned. She too felt star-struck. It was all happening so quickly.

"Oh, darling." Greta stopped and looked at Zane. "These aren't like walking on clouds, they're like walking on rainbows. You have discovered something here with Winter Shoes. Really something."

Heat radiated through Megan.

Greta Breen likes my shoes!

"I love them," Greta added smiling at Megan.

Greta Breen loves my shoes!

Megan smiled back. "I'm so glad. I take comfort as seriously as design and leaving a low carbon footprint." She paused. "I'm also passionate about fair trade, and organically sourced materials are used whenever possible."

"We need more like you," Greta said. She picked up another pair of heels that were twice as high and dotted with tiny butterflies. "So pretty." She turned to Zane. "But I'm going to have to come back tomorrow. I have an urgent appointment. Wrap these and the ones I'm wearing for now and I'll schedule a fitting into my diary. I have The Sparkling Stars Awards at the weekend and I had picked a pair of Michael Kors to wear with my Roberto Cavalli dress, but I'm going to do a last minute switch."

Zane sucked in a breath. "Really?"

"Yes really, I'm not going to another award ceremony and getting papped looking like I have a cat's ass for a mouth because my feet are on fire. I want style and comfort, which means I want Winter Shoes. No, scrap that, I *need* Winter Shoes."

Megan could hardly believe what she was hearing. Greta

Breen was going to wear her shoes to the ceremony that she herself was attending. How exciting.

"Of course, of course," Zane said, beaming. "You have my personal number, call me when you're on your way and I'll be at your service."

"Oh you're always so sweet to me." Greta removed the shoes and put her own pair back on. She stood and walked up to Megan. "Charmed to meet you. You've gained a fan today." She leaned in and created a flamboyant air-kiss by Megan's ear.

"Thank you for coming," Megan said. "And for your support."

"No thanks required, except maybe from my feet when they actually enjoy a night out instead of struggling through an event." She clicked her fingers at the man by her side. "Lars, come on, put that drink down, we're off."

He nodded once, set the half empty glass aside then trailed behind her. The security guy stuck his head out of the door, checked, gave the all clear, then they were gone.

"Wow," Brendon said, sitting heavily in the chair Greta had used. "I was just dumbstruck. She's amazing, such a star. I lost the ability to speak."

"She can be a bit of a diva at times," Zane said, helping himself to a drink. "But mostly she's all about being the best actress she can be and looking the best she can."

"Is Lars her husband?" Megan said, trying to recall from the gossip magazine if Greta was married.

"No, not at all. He's the male version of a handbag dog," Zane said then looked at Gucci and laughed. "Though he never looks very happy about it. I guess she pays him to be at her beck and call."

Megan straightened a pair of shoes on the display. The door clicked again as it was opened. She turned to see who their next guest was.

Georgie.

"What the...?" Megan felt a rush of adrenaline attack her system.

"Happy birthday," Georgie said, dropping a soft leather holdall on the floor and spreading her arms. She had a huge grin on her face and wore a floppy fabric hat.

"Oh my God." Megan clasped her hand over her mouth. Was Georgie real? Had her best friend really flown half way around the world to see her?

Brendon stood and rested his hand on Megan's arm. "Did you really think she was going to miss this? Your launch, your first day of global domination?"

"And the first day of your thirty first year." Georgie grinned.

Megan rushed into her arms, hugging her tight and still hardly able to believe this turn of events. She'd thought the day couldn't get any better yet it had just gone off-the-scale amazing.

James.

No she mustn't think of James

She couldn't have everything.

No one had all of their dreams come true.

A small sob hiccupped from her chest.

"Hey, hey," Georgie said, stroking Megan's hair. "You okay?"

Megan pulled back. "I'm just so happy you're here. I'm bowled over that you've done this for me."

"Not entirely selfless," Georgie said, her eyes misting a little. "I did kinda want a holiday in LA too. You guys are having all the fun and I'm missing out."

"Well not anymore," Megan said. "Oh, I'm so excited."

"Ladies, ladies," Brendon said, joining in the hug. "Please, no tears, think of the mascara smudges. No one wants to walk in here and see pandas."

Megan took a deep breath. Brendon was right, another guest could appear at any time.

"Ah, so you're the famous Georgie," Zane said, handing her a glass of champagne.

"Yes, and you must be Zane." She took the drink and knocked back half in one go.

"The very one," Zane said.

"Nice to meet you," Georgie said, licking her lips, "and thanks, you know, for being the catalyst to all this. Winter Shoes has been waiting to break out for a few years and it seems, looking around here at least, that it's finally on the map."

"We're all about getting talent on the map and there's only one street on that map for designers in LA and that's Rodeo Drive, baby."

"And we have two celebs already lined up to wear Megan's shoes for events. Greta Breen and Amanda Rush."

"No way!" Georgie's eyes widened. "That's awesome." She turned to Megan. "But seriously, you have to tell me about Tate Simmons. What's going on with you two? When will I meet him? Do you have any souvenirs of his at your place yet? Hat, socks, toothbrush maybe?"

Megan laughed. "No I don't, he's only been round once and that was to show us the place."

"But you have been seeing him?"

"Yes, well, sort of…"

"She's still missing Hot Guy," Brendon said with a dramatic sigh.

"Who is Hot Guy?" Zane asked, looking particularly interested.

"A big wig director who stole our Megan's heart over the summer and is now here, in LA," Brendon said.

"I still can't believe it," Georgie said. "What are the chances of James showing up to the place you ran to get away from him?"

"Well it wasn't him really I was getting away from. Dylan was the one creeping me out."

"Yes, you're right." Georgie gave a shudder. "He's lost the plot."

"It's fate," Zane said, throwing his arms in the air. "That's what I call it. That's why your Hot Guy is here."

Brendon smiled at him. "You're an old romantic at heart, aren't you?"

"Well, I've been called worse things," Zane said then pouted and fluttered his eyelashes at Brendon.

"So does that mean you're not going out with Tate because of James?" Georgie asked, looking confused.

"Well no, I've just been busy and so has he, doing this lifeguard show. We went for lunch, though, and of course we have the award ceremony coming up."

"Ah, yes, that."

"You will still be here, won't you?" Megan asked, a sudden fear washing through her that Georgie might only be staying a few days.

"Yes, I'll be here. I've got a flight back in ten days. Couldn't leave Tom any longer or put wedding arrangements and work on hold for a full two weeks."

"That's fine, in fact it's more than fine, it's perfect," Megan said, rubbing her hands together. "We have so much to show you and talk about."

The front door opened again.

"Oh my, oh my. Knock me down with a feather and tickle me all over," Brendon said. "Look at that."

Megan saw what appeared to be a just an enormous bunch of flowers squeezing through the door. They were white and cream and wrapped in pink tissue and paper. As they came closer she saw that all of the tiny cream roses were all studded with crystals.

"Looking for a Megan Rose Winter," the delivery man said from behind them.

"Yes, that's me," Megan said.

Brendon took the flowers, staggering slightly under their weight.

"Who are they from?" Georgie asked.

James? No, that's crazy.

"I don't know. Mum, Dad and Olivia maybe?" Megan thought of her family who'd said the evening before how proud they were of her Rodeo Drive achievement.

"Well have a look," Zane said, scribbling on the delivery pad. "We need to know."

Megan plucked the large pink envelope from the centre of the bunch. The whole thing smelt divine and filled her nostrils. She opened the card that had *Megan* scrawled on the front.

Happy Birthday my little star shoe designer. I hope the launch goes real well. Looking forward to having a special time with you on Saturday. I just know you're going to look fantastic on my arm.

Tate xxxxx

8

Megan slipped her feet into the finale of the outfit she'd been looking forward to wearing all week—a pair of bespoke sunset-red jewel-encrusted heels with glitter souls and delicate ankle straps. They not only completed the A-list look but were also a dream to wear, as Greta Breen had said herself.

She turned a circle in front of the mirror, admiring the cut of the LA Hype fishtail dress and the way it hugged her curves like a second skin. She might be the odd one out in Hollywood for having a shape but she was embracing that fact. If not being a shapeless stick was good enough for Marilyn, then it was certainly good enough for her.

And she *felt* good. She'd been rushing about organising new stock for LA Hype. Zane was struggling to keep up with demand. Enid, her manufacturers and courier company were all flat out and more LA stores were enquiring about stocking her products. She hoped that many more stores around LA—only the best of course—would soon be launching her wares. It was completely thrilling to think that people were clamouring to put their feet in her designs this many miles away from where she'd sat in London designing them.

And the icing on the cake was that Georgie was here to be part of the whole thing. She wasn't just an ace human resource manager, she was an ace manager all round, and even though it was her holiday, she had mucked in with the work.

Megan had treated her two best friends to an amazing meal at Chic the night before to say thank you for their support, but that was only the start. She had plans to draw up a proper contract for Brendon so that he'd be her official

PR manager, and Georgie, well, she'd take her, and Tom, on a chartered yacht around the Caribbean when she made her first million.

"Oh, Megan." Georgie stepped into the bedroom. "You look…"

"Too red?" She glanced at her cheeks in the mirror worried the makeup artist who'd been to the house had overdosed on blusher.

"No, well, yes, red, but not your cheeks, just… You look amazing. A vision of perfection from head to toe. Tate will not be able to resist you."

A tiny nugget of excitement was knocked off the pillar of anticipation roaring through Megan. Much as Tate was gorgeous, and the diamanté-speckled flowers had been the most extravagant floral gesture she'd ever received, she still wasn't convinced she wanted to end up in his arms after the ceremony. As for his bed…she was pretty damn sure she didn't want that to happen. It was way too soon.

"Oh come on, perk up," Georgie said, taking her hands.

"I am, I'm fine." Megan smiled and squeezed Georgie's fingers.

"It will all be fine."

"I know, but, well me and Tate. It's not quite…"

"Sitting comfortably, I know. But go with him. That's what you decided."

"I know."

"And enjoy a red-carpet moment. How many human beings on the planet actually get that?"

"I know, I know, nought-point-nought-one percent or something."

"Exactly."

"I'm just —"

"Worried that you're using him?"

"Well no, but…yes." Megan glanced at the floor. "But I do like him. He's particularly easy on the eye and he seems like a nice enough bloke when you look past his self-centredness."

"We went through this last night. If you're using him he's only using you to shove a finger up at this rock chick he's just broken up with. He's gone from one extreme to the other. Switched from messed-up, druggie tattoo girl to sweet English rose. It's a win-win for him. He pisses her off and the tattle mags get pages of speculation. As they're fond of saying here, no publicity is bad publicity."

"I guess." Megan picked up the earrings her parents had sent for her birthday. They were tiny gold butterflies and so understated and elegant they complemented the outfit in just the way she'd hoped. It would be perfect if her Mum and Dad saw pictures of her at the awards and she was wearing their gift.

"It's all cool." Georgie grinned. "Go with it. You're going to have the time of your life, and it's what you always wanted, fame and fortune."

"I know." Megan looked at her best friend. She looked incredibly pretty with her hair piled up in a loose knot and her skin slightly tanned from a week in the sun. "You're right."

"I'm always right." Georgie hugged her. "But right now...I don't want to crease you."

Megan laughed. "I'm not that delicate."

"No, but your dress is and you are late." She glanced at her watch. "The driver is here to collect you and Tate will be waiting so you can exit the car together onto the all-important carpet."

Megan pulled in a deep breath. This was it. The moment had arrived. It was time to walk the walk and talk the talk.

She carefully placed the slim purse with a gold chain strap over her shoulder and headed from the room.

Within minutes, and with lots of advice, kisses and hoots of delight from Brendon and Georgie, Megan got in the car. Her driver pulled away from the kerb towards Tate's home.

She fiddled with her earrings, brushed at a faint crease on her dress and plucked at invisible lint. She was starting to get hot and hoped her nose wasn't beginning to shine, so she asked the driver to turn up the air con. Her stomach rumbled. She'd forgotten to eat before the event and now she was hungry.

Luckily Tate lived only a half mile along the Pacific Highway towards Malibu and soon they were entering the gated front drive of his beachside villa. Megan admired the old wooden panelling that had been weathered by salt and the low porch that she knew must lead to a home with a particularly spectacular view of the ocean. All the homes along this stretch were like that. Understated at the front with amazing decks and steps down to some of the most expensive sand frontage in the world.

Tate must have been waiting for them because he appeared the instant the car drew to a halt. Wearing a pristine tuxedo and with his hair in his trademark 'surfer-dude' style, he hopped into the car.

"Hey, gorgeous," he said, pressing a quick kiss to Megan's cheek. "You look awesome in red."

"Thank you." He smelled of his usual strong aftershave and she noticed that despite the smart clothes, he still wore his medley of leather thong-style bracelets. He also had a ring embossed with an ugly silver skull on his right index finger.

"Shouldn't take long to get there," he said, snapping his suit jacket straight and settling back. He ran his finger over his eyebrows, first the right then the left.

"No, hopefully the traffic will be okay." Megan felt weirdly distant from him, though she hoped that would pass as the evening progressed. Maybe they were both just nervous. "Thanks again for the flowers on my birthday, they were something special."

"Well *you're* special, honey." He flashed her a grin.

"I don't know about that."

"Of course you do. You're here with me now and that makes you special. We'll be strutting our stuff outside the Dolby Theatre in a few minutes." He paused. "Though I'll apologies in advance if I get side-tracked by reporters. That often happens. They have a ton of questions about this and that, next movie, next project, recent article, rumour, you know what it's like. I just have to smile and nod and take it in my stride. Soon as that's done – and just hang around off camera until I've done my stuff – we'll head inside and the real fun starts. A few drinks, check out who else is there who is anyone and the awards get into full swing." He rubbed his hands together. "And I don't know about you but I'm ready for a drink. It's been a long week wrapping up this damn documentary with your buddy James. Long days, take after take until we..." He paused and did air brackets. "Get. It. Right." He shook his head. "Yeah, I'm ready for a damn drink."

"Oh, okay." Megan glanced out of the black-tinted windows. She wasn't bothered about a drink at all. She just wanted to get there now. The thought of all the reporters and journalists who'd be hanging around waiting for them made her nervous.

"Hey, hey," Tate said, taking her hand. He brushed his lips over her knuckles. "Take a chill pill. It's all cool."

She looked at him and smiled. "Yep, I know. This is all new for me, that's all."

"I know you're not a pro like me but look at this as a starting point. If all goes to plan, you'll be the star of every fashion catwalk around the world, your shoes being worn by the best of the best, so you may as well get used to it." He gave her hand a squeeze and kept it in his. "Attention, that is."

Before long the famous curved rooftop of the Dolby Theatre came into view and the limo pulled up – as directed by officials – against the red carpet.

"This is it," Tate said. "Show time. Let's rock and roll." He licked his lips and checked his hair then produced a dazzling smile.

The door opened and the sound of the crowd poured into the car – people calling his name, the click of photographs being taken and the low rumble of a brass band.

Tate stood and straightened his jacket. He then stepped forward and gave a casual wave.

The crowd roared.

A security man with a stern expression and black sunglasses leaned into the car and offered his hand to Megan.

She took it gratefully and rose from the car as elegantly as she could. Her dress settled around her ankles and she pulled in a deep breath. Her ears were ringing with the noise of cheers. Tate's arrival had caused quite a stir.

The crowds seemed to be a flash of bulbs and heaving mass of people. For a moment, she was a little disorientated and not sure where to look.

"If you could just step forward please, ma'am." The security guy gestured to a spot just behind Tate.

"Yes, of course." Megan stepped away from the car, clutching her purse.

Tate seemed to suddenly remember she was there and turned and smiled. "This way." He took her hand and led her halfway down the red carpet.

Megan plastered a smile on her face and held onto him. It was strange to see such a sea of faces all looking her way — curious, jealous and judgemental eyes all scrutinised her.

"Tate, Tate, over here. Sunshine News. Can you spare us a moment?" An earnest looking reporter waved a fluffy microphone towards them. He had floppy black hair and a moustache.

"Sure." Tate dropped Megan's hand and stepped up to him.

"Odds are on for *Run to Me* to win tonight, how do you feel about that?"

"Very excited, though nothing can be taken for granted. I've got some stiff competition." Tate broadened his smile for the cameraman who stood behind the reporter.

"And is it true that you and Titiana are officially over?"

Megan saw Tate's shoulders rise a little and for a moment his smile twitched. "I think tonight is about celebrating great story telling and cinematography, not my love life."

"So who is the beauty at your side now?" The camera swung Megan's way.

Megan did her best to keep her smile consistent even though her face felt stiff and her heart was pounding.

"Oh, just a friend." Tate stepped back, slipped his arm around Megan's waist and dragged her near. "A *good* friend."

"What's your name, honey?" another reporter called, thrusting forward a microphone.

"Yeah, who are you?" said another.

"Come on, let's go..." Tate pulled Megan away, and they headed down the red carpet. "Just smile and wave," he said under his breath, his broad grin not wavering. "Smile and wave."

Megan did as he'd asked. Her cheeks felt like they were vibrating with nerves and her knees were wobbly. But she was okay and she held her head high.

"Tate, Tate, over here. Pose with your lovely new lady."

Tate paused and swung them both to the right. He tipped his head to hers and pulled her even closer, making them look very intimate and desperately in love.

Megan gripped her purse a little tighter, wondering if she'd be given a chance to speak to this reporter and tell him her name.

"Let's get in there," Tate said, raising his hand to a group of fans holding pens and pads. "I'll do some signing later, guys."

They entered through a curtain of cool, the air con raining down on them. Megan paused for a moment as her eyes adjusted to the dim light. They were then ushered forward into a larger room with majestic and intricately carved doors.

"This way," Tate said, slackening his grip on her and taking a flute of champagne from a waiter who'd rushed up to them. He knocked back a big gulp.

Megan also took a drink and held it steady as they entered

the main reception room. Again she paused and took in her surroundings. The ceiling was domed and had several huge sparkling chandeliers hanging from it. The walls were draped in red silk and ten-feet high replicas of the awards stood pride of place against the back wall. Each award— shaped like a shooting star—shone brightly

And what an audience! Many faces she recognised from the world of showbiz. These were not just any old celebrities either, they were big names from movies and hit TV shows. Megan imagined they'd all be hoping to leave with one of the treasured awards, be it for acting, cinematography, producing, direction or soundtrack, there was an award for everything going on, so Tate had said.

She spotted Greta Breen, who glanced Megan's way. She held up her flute in greeting and smiled.

Megan nodded and smiled back, thrilled to see someone who actually had an idea who she was.

"Drink up," Tate said. "This is just the start. A mingle in here then we'll go in for the awards. They don't usually hang around at these things, it's all done and dusted by ten, so you've got to make the most of it." He swapped his already empty glass for a fresh one.

Megan had only taken one sip of hers.

She took a step to the side to let a glamorous woman in a full-length, billowing dress glide past.

Her elbow nudged something solid, a person, and she turned to apologise. "Oh, I am sorr…"

Her heart stuttered. Her mouth dried. Her spine seemed to weaken.

Before her stood…James.

James Carter.

Her James.

Dressed in a stunning black suit complete with bow tie and cummerbund, he looked every inch a Hollywood star, even though he was on the other side of the camera. His hair was neat—she guessed he'd had it trimmed for the event, and he was clean shaven. She could smell him too, his usual gorgeous scent that reminded her of the times they'd spent together.

"Megan," he said. A flash of surprise crossed his face but he quickly dampened it down.

"What...what are you doing here?" Megan asked. She was aware of Tate again slipping his hand around her waist. It was a possessive hold and his hand felt too big and his skin too hot even through the material of her dress.

James frowned and his lips tightened. "I'm up for an award, Best Director."

"Oh." How could she not have known that? Oh yeah, she'd been too busy with Winter Shoes to check all the details of the evening. She wanted to kick herself for being so slack. Brendon and Georgie would be exasperated with her. Several times over the past week, as Brendon had flitted from job to job, he'd told her to do her homework on the awards. "That's good then, to be nominated."

"Yes, I think so." James glanced at Tate who was grinning smugly at him.

Megan wriggled a little, trying to move away from Tate but he kept her close.

"And I think it's good that Megan is here with me," Tate said, "as my date."

Megan inwardly groaned. She knew she'd blown her chance with James but it seemed her fears in the Japanese restaurant that Tate would use their past relationship to wind his new director up had been well founded.

She saw James' jaw clench, as though he was gritting his teeth, and a muscle flexed in his cheek.

But what did he care really? They were over. He hadn't answered her calls or even given her a chance to explain.

So why should she explain this?

She had her reasons for being at Tate's side and her reasons for being in LA and none of them had anything to do with James.

But I wish they did.

"Don't you think she looks beautiful?" Tate said to James.

"The perfect English rose."

Megan looked into James' eyes. She'd always loved their depth, the way he seemed to see into her soul and make the rest of the world fade away. When his attention was on her, when he was looking at her, it was like she was the only woman on the planet, nothing else seemed to matter.

"She does indeed look..." James let his gaze slip down her body then back up to her face.

Megan's belly trembled and she gripped the stem of her drink so hard she had to slacken her fingers for fear of shattering the glass.

"She does indeed look," James repeated. "Incredibly beautiful, you should be proud to have her on your arm, Tate." He paused and swallowed. "You're a lucky man." He didn't take his eyes from Megan's face even though he was speaking to Tate.

"Yeah, I sure am." Tate chuckled and drained his drink.

"Thank you," Megan said, her voice a whisper. She cleared her throat. "And are you here with anyone, James?" She braced for a supermodel to suddenly join him, drape herself against his body and kiss his cheek.

"Hey, James, come on we're..." James' assistant appeared at his shoulder. His cheeks were a little red and he looked excited. He too was dressed in a smart black suit.

Megan tried to recall his name. She'd met him at the studio in London and James had talked about him several times. *Grant. Yes, that's it. Grant.*

"Oh," Grant said, his gaze settling on Megan then switching to Tate. "I see." He grinned. "You two are..." He flicked his fingers between them then looked at James.

"Yes," Tate said, pressing a kiss to Megan's head. "We are."

"We're together at the ceremony, that's all," Megan added, pleading with her eyes for James to believe that's all they were. Just here, one date. Okay it was high profile and the papers would have a field day with it but still... other than this, there wasn't anything more than lunch and a bunch of flowers between them.

"Well I have to go." James tilted his chin. "Enjoy your evening, Megan." He nodded at Tate. "Good luck."

"Yeah, you too, buddy. Hope your wildest dreams come true." He chuckled.

James and Grant turned and walked from the room, joining in with the rest of the crowd who were slowly being ushered to the auditorium.

Megan studied his lean but solid frame. He could model the perfect way to wear a tux. His shoulders were wide, his waist neat and his legs long. He moved with such grace, almost regally, as if confidence was something that he was never going to run out of. It was one of the things that had attracted her to him in the first place — the way he walked, the way he always seemed lost in thought, almost brooding, and how he was so self-assured. He was dark, mysterious, and right now, she'd give it all up to be the woman at his side, *his* date.

Tate was on another glass of champagne and engaged in a conversation with an older man she couldn't put a name to. He let his arm fall from her waist and she started for the theatre to find their seats.

One hour later, after much fanfare that included long-winded introductions of the judges, several short films and the latest number one hit from Trouble Brothers, the awards were finally starting.

Megan settled back and crossed her legs. They had a good spot near the stage and only a few seats in. She guessed that was because Tate was up for an award and it made it easy for him to get out and collect his trophy if he won.

She just hoped he'd be able to walk. He'd snagged another drink on their way out then he'd polished off her remaining half glass of champagne too.

"And so," the host of the evening started, "without further

ado, we're going straight to Best Supporting Actress in a TV series. The nominations are Melanie Crouch for her role in *Tame*, Sarah Jennings for her role in *One Plus One* and Naomi Reed for her role in *Seven Nights in Summer*."

As he read out each name, the actresses' faces flashed across a large screen behind him.

"And the winner is…"

Megan found herself holding her breath.

"Naomi Reed for her role in *Seven Nights in Summer*."

There was a burst of applause and a camera panned to the winner so her reaction was available for all to see on the screen.

She shook her head in shock then was kissed by her neighbour. She stood and made her way to the stage, shaking hands and smiling as she went. Her eyes were misty and she clutched a handkerchief.

"Glad she got it," Tate said loudly. "I can't bear Sarah Jennings."

Megan turned to him surprised. "What?"

"Yeah, she's a two-faced bitch."

"Shh…" Megan glanced around, hoping no one could hear or was recording their conversation.

"What?" Tate said, still clapping. "No one can hear."

"But they might."

"They won't." As he spoke, he breathed on her.

He smelled strongly of alcohol and she wished she could give him some water, or even better, a coffee.

The actress took to the stage and air-kissed the host as she took her award.

"Thank you so much," she said shakily into the microphone. "This means the world to me. But I couldn't do it without my family and friends." She paused and gave a dramatic sigh. "I know there are more for me to thank and I should have written a speech but you've caught me out here. Being up against Sarah and Melanie, I really didn't think I stood a chance. Again, thank you." She stepped away.

"Well isn't she a delight," said the host, stepping forward. "Well deserved." He pulled another envelope from his pocket. "Now onto Best Director for an investigative documentary. In this category we have Ben Tru for *The War Inside*, James Carter for *Poor Choices* and Reginald Waters for *Enough Charity.*"

Megan's heart rate picked up just from hearing his name and when she saw his face on the screen, handsome as ever, her stomach clenched.

She glanced around, wondering again if she would be able to spot him. But she couldn't. There were simply too many people in the room.

"And the winner is..." the host said, peeling open the envelope. "James Carter for *Poor Choices.*"

The crowd exploded in applause. A few people in front of her stood.

She clapped so hard her hands hurt.

A few more people stood, then more, like a ripple the audience rose and soon everyone was standing, including Megan herself.

Except for Tate, who was still sitting.

"Tate," she said, frowning at him.

He rolled his eyes and stood. He was clapping slowly, as if bored.

Then she saw him. James. Her James.

No, he's not mine. I can't keep thinking that.

He strode onto the stage, making short work of the distance. He shook hands with the host, took hold of the award and turned to the audience.

The clapping subsided and gradually everyone sat.

"Wow," he said, leaning into the microphone. "What a noise you lot make." He smiled.

There was a murmur of laughter.

He took a deep breath and scanned the audience. "I want to say thank you not just to the judges for this award but also to my studio for the opportunity to follow my passion. I believe in transparency, justice and freedom of speech.

With a camera—Grant, you're my top man." He pointed into the audience. "And given the financial support to create documentaries that explore the darker side of humans is really and truly my life calling. *Poor Choices* isn't the first and won't be the last exposé my team and I create. Where there is something that needs to be brought to the world's attention, we'll be there."

Megan thought she'd burst with pride. He looked so passionate, so handsome and so in control up on that stage. Commanding the attention of an entire theatre seemed effortless to him, as though he was born to be there, born to lead.

James held up the award. "This isn't just a win for me, it's for my team and all of the people in our documentaries who need their stories to be told. Without recognition of their bravery to be filmed and without the solid support of the industry, it would be impossible to carry on." He pressed his free hand to his chest. "Long may the fight for justice, peace and freedom continue." He stepped back.

"Smug asshole," Tate muttered.

Megan gasped and stared at him. *Of all the...*

Again the crowd roared and this time instead of a gradual standing ovation, everyone jumped up to their feet.

Megan decided to ignore Tate. She didn't want his drunken mutterings ruining the moment.

James won!

He walked back to his seat, shaking a few hands on his way. He had to come within a few feet of Megan and as he did so, his eyes landed on her.

Her breathing hitched. She hoped he could tell by her face how proud she was, how pleased she was for him.

Within a second he was gone, swallowed into the crowd and the shadows behind her and his face was lost from the big screen.

9

"Well I think we can safely say James Carter was a popular winner in that category," the host said with a smile as the audience calmed. "And so he should be, and, ladies, that British accent…" He winked. "What do you think?"

There were several whoops and another brief round of applause.

Not just the accent, what about the eyes, the smile, the body, the principles of a true gentleman…

Tate reached for her hand and squeezed.

She pulled it away and pretended to be checking something in her bag.

He frowned and shifted in his seat. His eyes were a little glazed.

Several more awards were read out. Best Film Director, Best Soundtrack, Best TV Series then Tate's award came around.

"Wish me luck," he murmured Megan's way.

"Absolutely," she said with a forced smile. Damn, she hoped if he did win he'd be able to manage a decent speech and not give the game away that he was pissed.

"Here we go, to one of the biggies," the host said, flashing a smile at the audience. "Time for Best Actor in a movie. The nominees are…" He opened the envelope then glanced at the big screen. "Rhet Newman for *Japan*, Bradley Callahan for *Upside Down*, and Tate Simmons for *Better off Dead*."

As Tate's name was read out, several catcalls filled the room. The female fans were clearly appreciative of his attendance.

He grinned and nodded and his reaction was caught on the big screen.

As soon as his image had gone, he straightened his tie and

rubbed his hands together. He bit on his bottom lip.

"And the winner is…Tate Simmons."

He turned to Megan with feigned surprise on his face then nodded and thanked the actor and his wife in front who turned and offered congratulations. He kept up the shocked expression throughout.

"Well done," Megan said as he stood. She smiled, knowing she would also likely be on the big screen as the cameraman was so close to them.

"Thanks, honey." He bent and pressed a solid kiss to her lips.

The action caught Megan by surprise and she sat there a little dumbly for a moment, aware only of the softness of his mouth and the way he loomed over her, holding her cheek in his palm.

He straightened and smiled, a soft smile, one that was full of love and adoration as he stroked her face with his thumb. It was as if she was the reason he'd won. The pillar of support at his side, the woman in his life. As though he couldn't have done it without her.

Damn, he's one heck of an actor.

As he turned and began to make his way to the stage, Megan shook her head slightly. He absolutely deserved that award, he'd just convinced an entire auditorium, likely the world, that they were a serious couple with a history, a future and an anchor of emotion holding them together. When in fact they were on nothing more than a second date—if you counted a swift lunch as the first, that was.

Her stomach clenched and a weight settled in her chest. If the final nail in the coffin on her and James hadn't long since been hammered in, then that would have done it for sure.

She clapped as Tate went onto the stage, pleased that he was walking in a straight line at least. He shook hands with the host, took his award and kissed it.

The audience were still clapping as he went up to the microphone.

She had to admit he looked the part, casually gorgeous and with not an ounce of humility. He'd wanted that award and he'd got it. Tate, it seemed, got what he wanted in life.

"Yo!" he called holding up the statue. "I did it!" He punched the air with his free hand. "I won."

There was another round of clapping and *whoops* from the audience.

"Thank you..." he said, running his fingers through his hair. It flopped back into its usual style. "For giving me this award, it's going to have pride of place in the bathroom." He laughed loudly. "With all my other awards...and there's lots..."

A polite rumble of humour filtered around the place.

"And," he said, "of course I have a list of people to thank. Mom, Dad, the director, and the boys at the Skids bar — Dirk, Matt, Greg, you all rock and we're going to get wrecked to celebrate this baby!" Again he kissed the trophy.

Megan hoped that was him finished. He was overexcited and loud, and people were smiling politely but also shifting in their seats a little uncomfortably.

The host took a step forward.

Tate ignored him.

"And of course nothing beats having a good woman at your side to make it all worth it." He pointed at Megan.

Her heart skipped a beat as her face flashed on the big screen. She smiled, sort of, and wished the cameraman would get out of her personal space.

"A good woman to keep me on the straight and narrow, and warm at night." Tate banged his fist on his chest. "This is for you too, babe. You're sweet and sexy and hot, and later on when we get home, I'm going to show you just how much I adore you by —"

"Well thank you, Tate Simmons," the host intercepted. "Please, give our winner a final round of applause." He started clapping and so did the rest of the audience.

Tate looked a bit put out for a split second then he waved, smiled and headed back stage ready to take his seat again.

Megan felt as if her skin was on fire. What the hell had he been about to say? It could have been any number of lewd, rude or damn right filthy things. As it was, what he had said had been suggestive enough. For God's sake, the most they'd done was have a chaste kiss.

"And that was our final winner of the evening," the host said. "It's been wonderful, and I thank you all for coming, the judges, and of course the viewers for watching. Let's keep on making great entertainment and I'll see you all next year."

Thank goodness for that.

The audience clapped and a few people stood and started moving about.

Megan glanced around. She didn't want to see Tate, she'd had enough of him for one evening. In fact, she'd had enough of him forever. He was a phony and a fake and she had no time for a man who thought it was okay to make out to the world they were sleeping together, that they were an item, when they weren't.

She stood. Beneath her long dress, her legs felt twitchy. As if they'd had a shot of adrenaline injected into the muscles. The urge to get the hell out of the Dolby Theatre was overwhelming — away from Tate, the mess that was left of her relationship with James and the damn cameraman who was still lurking.

She moved to the aisle. "Excuse me," she said to the camera guy.

"What's your name?" he asked, finally dropping the lens and peering at her curiously.

Megan ignored him. Instead she clutched her bag and hurried up the aisle. Actors and their guests were milling about slowly but she didn't linger, she rushed past them. The call of the night air was like a siren, the heat of the theatre suddenly too much. She couldn't breathe, she had to go. Leave it all behind.

She rushed past Greta Breen and her companion, her focus on the door. Once out in the lobby, she spotted a sign for a side exit and walked as fast as she could towards it. Her heels clacked as she strutted past several security guys.

"Can I go out this way?" she asked one of them who was guarding a doorway.

He looked at her through narrowed eyes. "Yes, ma'am."

"Thanks."

He opened the door, and she stepped out, pleased to see that she was in a side street and not at the front of the building where all the paparazzi were lurking.

It was almost dark now and she could see the bright lights of Hollywood Boulevard. Perhaps if she headed that way and walked down a block she could grab a cab?

She set off at a brisk pace, clutching her bag. The air, though hot, was fresher and it felt like it was travelling right to the base of her lungs. Each step she took away from the Dolby Theatre, away from Tate, made her feel slightly better.

But only slightly. She was still seething with his presumptuous and suggestive comments about her.

She heard someone behind her, but didn't turn. Instead she hurried on, taking a right once on the main street and praying for a cab.

Luckily she saw one, held up her hand and sent a thank you up to the heavens when it pulled over. The last thing she wanted was to be recognised as the woman with Tate Simmons and have to start fielding questions. Maybe another time she'd have coped, but right now her emotions were in shreds.

"Where to?" the driver asked as she slid in and shut the door.

"Venice Beach, please."

"Sure thing." He flicked on his meter and pulled away from the kerb.

Megan blew out a breath and hugged her arms around herself. How the hell had she ended up in this position? She needed Brendon. She needed Georgie. They'd say the right things, she was sure of it. They'd calm her nerves, tell her it was all going to be okay.

She stared at the entrance to the theatre as they navigated past. It sparkled and shone with brilliant white spotlights. Herds of people stood behind barriers, and flags flapped in the breeze.

Tate would be looking for her now. He'd have gone back to the seat, found her gone then set about searching.

Would he be mad? Would he care?

As they headed west down the hill, Megan pictured his face. A face that was beyond beautiful but hid an inside that really didn't match the image he projected. He might be mad that she'd gone but only because it made him look like he no longer had a date. That he was alone. It wouldn't be because he wanted to be with her. Missed her.

She hoped one of his agents or mates would find him and give him some coffee and keep him out of the way of cameras until he sobered up.

She clicked her tongue off the roof of her mouth. He hadn't given her a chance to even say who she was, she was nameless. The press had asked her but he'd steered her away. He'd talked about Winter Shoes maybe getting some publicity but that had been furthest from his thoughts. Not that she was bothered now — perhaps it suited her to be anonymous after that disastrous speech.

Her phone beeped and she retrieved it.

Brendon.

You okay, sweetpea?

She quickly replied.

On my way home. Alone.

Within a second a response came back.

We'll be waiting. XXXX

Thank goodness for her friends. They'd have seen the

whole thing on TV and would know exactly how she was feeling. She wouldn't even have to explain.

"Whereabouts in Venice Beach?" the driver asked.

Megan peered out of the window to get her bearings. She could just make out the beach through a small gap in the houses and figured they were halfway between Santa Monica and her new home.

"Here is fine," she said, sitting forward and reaching into her purse. Suddenly she felt like a walk along the meandering path that ran parallel to the Pacific Ocean. It would do her good to sift through her thoughts as the ocean breeze caressed her.

The car pulled over and she handed twenty dollars to the driver.

"Have a good evening now," he said.

"Thanks, you too."

She stepped out and scooped up her dress. It wasn't usual attire for a late night beach walk but she didn't think anyone would notice in LA. People did a whole host of crazy things that didn't draw a second glance.

She headed towards the beach. A car drew up behind her and she heard voices then a door slam. On and on she went, breathing deep and loving the feel of the fresh air on her face. Her heels clicked and echoed around the houses but as she reached the sidewalk and felt sand under the soles, the echoes stopped.

Except they didn't. She could still hear footsteps. Fast. Running.

Her heart skipped a beat. Someone was running towards her.

She sped up, broke into a run, cursed the fact that she couldn't go quicker.

Someone was chasing her. Hunting her down.

She glanced over her shoulder, saw the figure of a man with wide shoulders.

"Shit…" She looked around frantically but the place was deserted. Just the roll of the waves, the empty beach and houses in darkness. "Oh God."

"Megan...wait..."

He knew her name? This man who was after her.

"Megan, for crying out loud, woman, wait."

James?

No, it couldn't be. She sped up. The footsteps behind her sped up. Why the hell would James be out here? It was her mind playing tricks on her, terror fooling her ears.

"Megan would you for once, just once, not run away from me, woman."

His words settled in her brain. It was James. Her James. He was here.

She wasn't about to be brutally attacked and murdered by a mad man.

She slowed.

He was close now, she could hear him breathing.

She stopped. Turned.

"James?"

"Yes, it's me. Sorry if I scared you."

"Well you did that all right." She let her dress pool around her feet and put her hands on her hips. Fear turned to indignation.

He drew to a halt about ten feet from her. His feet hip-width apart and his arms hanging at his sides, fists clenched. A shard of light from a nearby street lamp sliced over his face. "I'm sorry, really I am, but I wanted to talk to you."

"You did?"

He does? Why?

"Yes." He huffed. "Trouble is, you always seem to be racing away from me, wherever we are and whatever happens, and I have no idea why you have this urge to escape."

"Well I didn't know it was you behind me..." Wouldn't any girl run if they thought a madman was after her?

"You thought it might be Tate." James almost spat his name.

"No, not for a minute. Tate is only interested in Tate. I

can't imagine that he'd leave an A-list ceremony to come and see if I'm okay." *Is that what you've done?*

"He seems pretty smitten with you." James folded his arms, the lapels on his jacket creasing slightly. "In love."

"He's a good actor." Megan looked out to sea as a particularly big roller crashed against the beach. "Which has just been proven by his award."

When she looked back at James, he'd taken a step closer to her.

"Explain," he said. There wasn't anger in his tone, just confusion. "He as good as told the world that he couldn't live without you."

Megan shook her head and stared into his eyes. "I hardly know him. We bumped into each other by chance, he helped me find somewhere to stay—"

"At his?" James looked aghast.

"No, no, not at his. Brendon and I are renting one of his mate's houses just a few blocks from here."

James' expression relaxed a little. "Oh, okay."

"And we've only done lunch once, that day I saw you on set, and then this evening we've been together as a date. Nothing more." Megan prayed James would believe her because it was the truth. There was nothing more between her and Tate. Whatever there had been was over. Even if being linked to him would do Winter Shoes good, she had her dignity and pride and there was nothing remotely appealing about hooking up with Tate Simmons. "There's nothing between me and Tate," she repeated quietly. "And whatever that nothing is, it's over. I'm free and single and not in any rush to jump into a life as Mrs Tate Simmons."

"You're definitely single?" He raised his eyebrows slightly.

"Yes."

"Good." He stepped up to her.

Megan caught her breath. He was tall and she had to tip her head back to look up into his face. His dark eyes sparkled at her, and he swept his tongue over his bottom lip. He was so handsome, so perfect and all she wanted to do was fall into his arms.

But she didn't. She stayed rooted to the spot. "Why is that good?" she whispered.

"Because..." He reached for her face and cupped her cheeks, slid his fingers into her hair. "It means I can do this."

He held her firm as he set a soft kiss on her lips.

Megan's breath hitched and she reached to hold onto his forearms.

He deepened the kiss, stroking his tongue into her mouth and slanting his head.

Megan opened up and let him in. He tasted of everything that had been missing in her life. Being held by him, kissed by him, made everything else okay. There was just them.

She pulled back a little and studied his face.

He wore a soft smile.

"You're not mad at me?"

"For what?"

"For...everything..."

"Well I think we probably need to clear a few things up but..." He swept his lips over hers again. "If this is our starting point, I reckon we'll be okay."

She felt like she was floating. He wasn't mad at her. He wanted to start again, from here. Hell, she could do with that.

"I'm so sorry," she said, her eyes misting.

"Hey, hey...there is nothing to be sorry about."

"But in London, I know what you saw, or what you think you saw, because Brendon came rushing in..."

"Brendon..." His eyes widened. "Oh..."

"And it was awful, thank goodness he did, because Dylan—"

"Dylan? Who is Dylan?" He frowned.

Megan sighed. Her belly clenched and the wind wrapped a lock of her hair over her cheek. She glanced at the sea again. "Perhaps we should go for a walk and I'll tell you who Dylan is and why I had to run away from London to

LA."

He stared at her for a moment then nodded. "Okay. We'll do that." He took her hand.

"Wait." Megan stooped and took off her shoes. "They'll get wrecked."

"And we definitely wouldn't want that." He took them from her, the slim straps looking particularly delicate hanging from his big fingers. "I'll carry them for you."

"Thanks."

Taking her hand again, he led the way to the sea front, to where the sand was hard enough to walk on but not being caught by the ebb and flow of the tide.

Megan scooped up her dress so that the base wouldn't get ruined.

"So Dylan," he said quietly.

"There's something you should know," Megan said. She swallowed, her throat felt tight. This was it, truth time.

"Oh..."

"I was engaged, to be married."

"Okay."

"To Dylan."

"The guy who was in your apartment that night?"

"Yes, that's him. I didn't invite him, I didn't want to see him, I don't, ever again, but he broke in."

"Broke in?"

"Yes...I'd...left the door on the latch by mistake and well, he'd been hanging about wanting to talk to me."

"I see."

"We didn't end well and he's always had hopes of us getting back together."

James was quiet.

"Which I don't want. He's controlling and domineering and used to hate Winter Shoes because it took me away from him."

"That's not very supportive."

"I agree." She paused. "The thing is, James..."

"What?"

120

Megan stopped and turned to him. This was it. The moment had come. This news about her past would either freak him out and he'd be the one hot-footing it away from her, or he'd see it had been her only option.

"What?" he asked again.

"I jilted him. At the altar. I was standing there in a white dress, all of our friends and family, the vicar, God, ready to marry him and I just...I just couldn't."

James nodded slowly.

"I saw a life of being held back, of being in his shadow and not achieving my dreams. I couldn't live with that, I wanted more. It was a shitty thing to do, I agree, but I just ran..."

"You ran." He shook his head and frowned slightly. "Why am I not surprised?"

"What else could I do? It was as if something was carrying me out of there, out of the church. I needed the freedom to be me and Dylan couldn't give me that." She bit on her bottom lip and studied James' face. Was he shocked, horrified, disgusted?

She couldn't tell.

"And he wasn't happy about that."

"No and I don't blame him, it was a terrible thing to do to a person, to humiliate him and — "

"Shh..." He pressed his index finger over her lips.

"What?"

"You don't have to explain anymore about that day."

"I don't?"

"No, I'm proud of you."

"You are?"

"Yes, you stood up for what was right for you. What you believed in. You fought oppression, fought for your rights as a woman and an individual, and I for one admire that very much."

Megan's head was spinning. James didn't hate her for what she'd done?

"Megan..." he said, releasing her hand and wrapping his

arms around her waist.

"Yes?" She rested her hands on his chest and his body heat radiated through his tuxedo jacket onto her palms.

"Will you come back to my place, now, so I can explain myself too?"

"What is there for you to explain?"

"You must have been furious with me for not returning your calls that last evening and morning in London."

She thought back to the hurt and confusion. All she'd wanted to do was explain and he hadn't given her the chance

"Well yes, I didn't understand it at all. I knew you'd seen Dylan but..."

"I can explain." He pressed another soft kiss to her lips. "Now text Brendon and tell him you'll be a bit later than expected so he doesn't worry about you, and we'll go to my place. It's only on the other side of the pier."

"You live on the other side of the pier." Megan glanced to her right. In the distance, the Ferris wheel was slowly spinning and the glittering lights of the amusements and stalls reached out into the inky ocean. "You live in Malibu?"

"Yes, London was nice but this...well let's just say I'd always hoped you'd see my other home."

10

They didn't walk to Malibu, instead James hailed them a cab from the main road.

"It's a bit too far to walk in the dark," he said as they hurtled along the Pacific Highway. "And I'm guessing you've had a long enough day."

"Yes, it's been busy." She looked at where their hands were joined, still hardly believing that this was how her evening at the Dolby Theatre had ended. "Hey, where is your trophy?"

"Grant has it, it's as much his as mine. Without him I'd be lost."

Megan smiled, she knew James was being modest. It was his ideas and know-how that created his award-winning documentaries. "Congratulations by the way. Well deserved."

"Thank you. I've heard that a lot this evening but coming from you it's extra nice."

A lovely warm glow flooded her veins. It was like that when she was with James. Everything felt special.

The cab slowed. Megan glanced out of the window. It was the second time she'd been to this neck of the woods in one day. Tate lived only a few hundred yards further on, but she decided not to mention that. Both she and James had had enough of Tate Simmons for one day.

"Just here, buddy," James said, indicating to the right.

The driver slowed and pulled onto a curved gravel driveway. Large wrought-iron gates swung open and a wide, one-storey white house was revealed.

"Very nice," Megan said. "Beats our little Venice Beach condo."

"It is nice, relaxing too with the sound of the waves." He

hopped out then held his hand out for Megan to take.

She stood, her heels, which she'd put back on, dipping into the gravel.

The cab pulled away and the gates shut again.

"Remote," James said, holding up his keys. "Makes life easy." He nodded at the house. "Come on in."

Megan took a deep breath. There was still more to talk about, more to say and explain. She tried not to think of Dylan these days and the way he'd made her feel not just hounded but also scared. They were feelings that were a million miles away right now and she didn't want to invite them back into her psyche.

"Wow," she said, stepping into the hallway.

James keyed in an alarm code and a muted beeping stopped.

"Do you like it?" he asked, flicking on a table lamp.

"Yes, it's lovely." Even from where she stood she could see the ocean sparkling in the moonlight. The vast majority of the house appeared to be open plan, with a modern kitchen complete with huge island, several low leather sofas angled at a TV and huge glass doors and windows that spanned the western side of the house. There was a large, lit decked area with what appeared to be a barbecue, pizza oven and hammock.

She toed off her shoes and wandered up to the doors, her bare feet silent on the cool tiles. "I've never seen a view like it."

"It's pretty special," James said, coming up behind her.

"And wow, is that a hot tub?"

"Yes, not that I ever have time to use it." He chuckled. "But maybe if you're here…" He stroked her cheek then set a soft kiss on the angle of her neck, just above where it met her shoulder.

She smiled. "Mmm…maybe."

He straightened. "Would you like a drink?"

"Yes, please."

"White wine? I have a nice one that's from Napa Valley,

not far from here."

"Perfect."

"Go out onto the deck. I'll be there in a moment." He stepped away.

Megan unlocked the door nearest to her and went into the night. The air was warm and the low rumble of the waves filled her ears. She stepped past a set of outdoor furniture and held onto the rail that supported the deck. Looking downward, she could see they were about twenty feet up and a set of wooden steps with a tall gate at the end led to the beach.

Santa Monica pier was to her left now and to her right the beach stretched into the distance.

"Here." James was at her side. He handed her a glass of white wine.

"Thanks."

"You want to sit?" He pointed at the soft chairs.

"I'm okay standing for a moment."

He nodded then took a sip of his drink.

"There is more," Megan said. "About Dylan."

"Oh?"

"Yes, he... Well he... It's why I'm here."

"What do you mean?" He frowned. "What did he do?"

"He was stalking me."

"What? Did you go to the police?"

"No, I didn't want to—"

"Why on earth not? He can't get away with doing that."

"I guess I just felt so bad for what I'd done to him. I just wanted it to end. I didn't want it to be any worse for him than it already was."

"But he can't do that to you, no one can." He paused. "And that's why he was in your house, why he'd broken in..." James set his drink on the table and paced across the decking. He stopped with his back to her and clasped his hands behind his head.

"James?"

"And I walked away." He spun around, pain slicing over

125

his handsome features. "I saw him in there with you and I turned and walked away. What a stupid fucking thing to do." He held his hands out, palms up, and faced her again. "God, you could have been hurt." He shook his head. "If you had been, I'd never have forgiven myself."

Megan was a little alarmed at his anger towards himself. "It's okay. You didn't know the full story, and besides, Brendon came quickly, he diffused the situation."

James stepped up close to her. He took her glass and set it aside.

"Megan."

"Yes?"

"I'm sorry. I judged. I saw you with another man, him kissing you—"

"Trying to kiss me!"

"Trying, whatever. I saw him there and presumed you had someone else in your life. I know we'd...you know, started something, but I didn't feel like I had any claim on you, much as I wanted you to just be mine we'd only just met."

"Please, don't blame yourself. It was Dylan's fault, no one else's."

James pressed his lips together and gave a small nod. "What else did he do, because I'm sure there's more?"

Megan reached up and pressed her palm to his jawline. "He sent me weird notes, silent calls, he harassed me from the shadows, lurked near my office day and night." She shook her head. "In the end, I just had to get away so I went to Heathrow and jumped on the first plane I could buy a ticket for which just happened to be—"

"LA."

"Yes, LA."

He smiled, just a little. "That's what I call fate."

"Because *you're* here?"

"Yes, and..."

"What?"

"When I came round that night, when I saw..." He

paused. "I was planning on asking you to come out to LA with me. I'd just had a phone call ordering me back to work on Tate's show and I thought maybe you'd enjoy hanging out here for a bit." He gestured to his home. "By the beach, in the sunshine, doodling and creating with a bit of space around you."

"You were? You did?"

"Don't look so surprised."

"But..."

"I like you, Megan, a lot. I have done from the first moment I saw you. And the thought of whatever it was we'd started ending so suddenly didn't sit well with me." He reached for her hand and pressed a kiss to the centre of her palm.

A tingle travelled up her arm.

"I don't do this whole dating thing very often," he said. "I simply don't have time, so when I meet someone I want to spend free time with I'm not going to give up easily."

Megan thought her heart would burst with joy. He wanted to spend time with her. He'd wanted her to be here, right here, with him.

She looked out to sea.

"What?" he asked.

"Why didn't you answer your phone? I tried to call, I left you a message."

He sighed and tucked a strand of hair behind her ear. "I was hurt, confused. I decided to sleep on it and when I woke up it was too late."

"What do you mean?"

"Well I went home, paced until the sun came up, not wanting to do anything drastic or while I was hot-headed, then I fell asleep exhausted. By the time I woke up and read your text I'd calmed down."

"So why didn't you call then?"

"I felt we needed to speak face-to-face. Whatever was between us deserved that. I respected what you'd told me, understood, sort of, but I needed to see into your eyes and hear it."

Megan nodded. "I can understand that."

"So," he went on, "I headed to the City and went to your office. It was about lunchtime by the time I arrived and your secretary was there."

"Enid."

"Yes, Enid. Anyway when I asked where you were she wouldn't tell me. Said she didn't know."

"She didn't. That was the truth."

He frowned. "Well I thought she was just being obstinate. What kind of secretary doesn't know where her boss is?"

"I'd hot-footed it out of there, dashed home, packed and then ran to the airport."

He half-chuckled. "I can believe that."

"Well obviously I didn't run all the way…" Megan smiled. "But you know what I mean."

"Yes, yes. I do." He pulled her close, settling her body against his. "And I'm glad we've finally got all that straightened out, even though it was a bit crazy back there for a bit."

"Tell me about it." She looked into his eyes — they were brimming with adoration, with understanding and… passion.

A tremble shot up her spine and she moulded herself closer to him. She swept her hands up his back. He'd removed his jacket and his crisp white shirt was thin so she could make out the contours of his muscles.

"Maybe…" he murmured, his lips almost touching hers, "we should make a pact."

"What's that?"

"No more running. No more misunderstandings."

"I can live with that." She grinned and touched the tip of her nose to his. "It gets exhausting running. I want to find somewhere to stop and exhale."

"Good, then maybe you'll consider stopping here, exhaling with me."

Her breaths were coming quickly, and she could feel the length of him pressing against her body. His arms were so thick and strong holding her, yet also gentle and loving.

"Do you remember that night?" he asked, slipping his hand down the curve of her lower back, lower still.

"Yes..." she whispered. She knew exactly what he was talking about.

"It was perfect. We were so..."

"In tune."

He smiled. "Yes, so in tune."

Megan went onto her tiptoes and kissed him, slipping her tongue between his lips.

James groaned and pulled her closer.

The sound of the waves faded, and she became less aware of the warm salty breeze tickling through her hair. There was only James. Her and James.

His lips left hers and he kissed over her cheek.

Megan tipped her head back and stared at the stars. Her body was buzzing, her desire to get closer, get skin on skin, was growing.

"You drove me crazy earlier," he murmured.

"Why?" She slid her hands around the back of his neck and through his soft hair.

"Seeing you in this damn sexy dress but not being able to touch you. And Tate—"

"Don't think about him. He's not in our lives anymore."

"Huh, I have to work with him." He nibbled her earlobe.

Megan squirmed a little. His breaths were hot and she wanted his mouth on hers.

"I couldn't stand the thought of him touching you, claiming you, telling the world you were his."

"I'm not."

He raised his head and looked down at her, a serious expression on his face. "Thank goodness."

She smiled. She had everything she needed in this man. Her body cried out for more. Could she? Should she?

Yes.

"James," she said, studying him. "I'm all yours, if you still want me."

"Do you even need to ask?"

"Well... Oh..."

He'd swung her up against his chest, one arm behind her thighs and one at her shoulders.

Quickly she looped her hands around his neck. "James." She giggled. "What are you doing?"

"Making you mine."

The way he'd spoken, with such dark determination and with such a sexy low timbre to his voice had goosebumps spreading over Megan. She wanted this passionate, principled man, to remind her what it felt like to be adored, to be with a gentleman.

He pushed through the screen door and into the living room.

Within seconds they were in what Megan assumed was his bedroom. Like the rest of the house she'd seen so far, it had huge windows and French doors that led to the decking. It also had an enormous low bed that was covered in white sheets and stacked with white pillows. The furniture appeared to be heavy, polished dark wood and a picture of the ocean hung on the wall opposite the bed.

He set her gently down on her feet and rested his hands on her shoulders. "Will you stay with me?"

She nodded. "Yes."

He kissed her, a hot, hungry kiss that sent need racing through her veins.

But all too suddenly he broke away. He applied pressure to her shoulders and urged her to turn, to face the windows and the ocean.

"This dress got a zipper somewhere?" he asked.

"Yes. At the back." She smoothed down the front, over her stomach. It was as if a swarm of butterflies were fluttering around in there. But she had no need to be nervous, this was James, her James, and she knew he'd make it all feel so good.

He found the zip and slid it down.

The dress slackened immediately and gaped around her

waist. She only wore knickers, a small white thong, as the dress had built in support.

James kissed her neck.

She melted against him and closed her eyes, happy to be lost in his touch. Warmth spread over her as the dress fell from her body, landing in a heap around her feet.

He pulled her closer, his palms skimming over her curves as he continued to kiss her neck.

Megan rested her hands on his forearms, felt the tendons and muscles shifting beneath.

"You've got too much on," he said, plucking at the delicate lace at the front of her thong.

"I don't think you can talk, Mister." She turned within his embrace and reached for his top button.

His mouth twitched in a half smile and he let his hands fall to his sides.

She was aware of him studying her, his gaze roaming her body, as she slowly undid each button on his dress shirt then tugged it from his waistband.

He quickly released the cuffs.

Megan slipped her hands from his chest to his shoulders, pushing the material off his body. He let it hang for a moment then tugged it off.

If he'd been enjoying looking at her then she was going to savour the moment of seeing James again. His wide chest had a sprinkle of chest hair and his shoulders were strong and lean. She tipped forward and kissed his right collar bone, slipped her palm over his pec then nibbled her way to his neck.

"You're so sweet…" he said, reaching into her hair.

He pulled a pin free and let it tumble to the floor with a small clatter.

He repeated the action, then again and again until Megan felt her carefully styled updo landing around her shoulders and neck.

"There," he said, slipping his fingers through the now free locks. "That's how I remember you in the bedroom."

He paused and grinned. "Tousled and naked."

Megan giggled. "Great look."

"Works for me." He suddenly spun her and tipped her onto the bed.

Her head landed on a pillow and the cool sheets caressed her body.

He settled on top of her, supporting some of his weight. "I've spent so long remembering our one time together, wishing I could have it all over again."

"Me too."

He smiled. "Good." He kissed her again.

Megan traced her fingers down his back and as he shoved at his trousers. They were in the way.

Soon they were both naked. Their bodies entwined.

"Megan..."

"What?" Her body was tense. She gripped his arms.

"I think...I love you..."

He entered her, and she gasped. "James."

"I didn't say it to hear it back," he said, touching his lips to hers.

"But..." Oh she wanted to say it, she really did. It was true. She loved him too.

"No, shh..." He began to move, rocking and building them up.

Megan wrapped her legs around the back of his, knotted her fingers in his hair and allowed bliss to race around her body.

She was hot.

He was panting.

The bed creaked.

Everything in her world was complete.

James loved her.

They were back together.

She clutched him closer. "Yes, yes."

Her body tipped into ecstasy. James joined her and they clung to each other, the moment sending her into a heady state of delirium. "James!"

"Megan…" They kissed, a wild, hungry kiss that spoke a hundred words about their needs and desires.

Eventually their frantic kissing subsided. Megan's breathing returned to normal and she relaxed her limbs.

James flopped to the bed next to her and reached for her hand. "You okay?"

"Yes, never better." She turned to him and smiled.

"Good." He traced a line from the hollow of her throat to her navel. "I think you'd better ring Brendon and tell him you're not coming home tonight."

"That's presumptuous," she said then giggled.

He pulled her close. "Not presumptuous, just preparing you, because that, baby, was just for starters."

11

James

James woke to the sound of the crashing ocean and with Megan in his arms. As far as he was concerned it was the most perfect start to a day he could ever remember. Buying this place and finding a good woman to join him was something he'd dreamed of. Sure he'd been on some dangerous journeys, thrived on adrenaline and had a burning ambition to tell the world about injustice, but right now, with this sweet woman in his arms—who he now knew he was in love with—that hit the spot for him.

She stirred and opened her eyes.

"Morning, gorgeous," he said then kissed her forehead.

She stretched her legs and arched her back, pressing herself against him. "Great place to wake up, I can hear the sea."

"Does it get any better?"

She smiled and slid her hand over his chest. "No, I really don't think it does."

"Mmm..." He pulled her closer. "I can think of one thing that might make it better."

She laughed, a cute little noise that filled his heart with joy. "I'm sure you can."

"Want me to show you?"

She pushed away. "Yes, you can show me in the form of breakfast. I'm starving. I didn't eat yesterday evening."

"What?" She hadn't eaten. She was tiny anyway—she couldn't afford to skip meals.

"I had a decent lunch but then got busy with orders and emails then it was hair and makeup and off to the ceremony and...well, you know the rest. Eating went out of the window."

"And you've used up a ton of calories in bed." He shook his head and grinned. "I'll fix this situation right now." He stood and pulled on boxers and a pair of soft jeans. "I'll cook the works, a proper English breakfast, not the green, wheat-free super-smoothies they have over here but eggs, bacon, toast, beans."

"That sounds wonderful," she said, pulling the sheet up to her chin and rolling her lips in on themselves.

He smiled. Just seeing her in his bed made him happy. He hoped she'd be back later so he could sleep cuddled up to her warm body again. He couldn't remember when he'd last slept so well — when he'd eventually fallen asleep, that was.

"I might just lie and listen to the waves for a few minutes more," she said, turning to face the window. "If you don't mind?"

"Of course not. Here, I'll open it up." He stepped up to the French doors and flung them wide. The ocean wind fluttered into the room, shifting the sheer white curtains and filling the room with fresh, salty air. "How's that?"

"Heavenly." She sighed and stared out to sea.

"It suits you." He stepped up to her.

"What does?" She set her gaze on him, her eyes drifting to his bare chest.

"Being here, in my bed...in my life. It suits you."

"I think so too."

He smiled. "I'll go make you that breakfast, no running away while I'm at it."

"I won't." She rolled her eyes. "I promise."

"Mmm..." He gave her a stern look.

"I promise." She reached for a small white cushion and threw it his way.

He caught it and laughed. "Good."

James wandered into the kitchen. A tune caught in his mind and he started to hum as he put on the kettle and checked out the contents of his fridge — not too bad at all.

Soon he had sausages sizzling under the grill, bacon frying, eggs beaten and wholemeal bread in the toaster. He sipped his tea and heard the shower going on.

Good, she'd found the en suite.

He glanced at the sausages and wondered if he had time to join her, but then he changed his mind. Nice as the thought was, this breakfast required his attention and Megan needed food.

He poked at the sausages then added the eggs to a pan and set about scrambling them. "Nearly ready," he called.

The shower went off. "Coming now."

He glanced at the bedroom door, spotted her walking barefoot and wrapped in just a towel across the room. Yep, he could cope with her staying like *that* while they ate.

"Smells good," she called.

"Yep, come and get it." He started to dish up.

She wandered from the bedroom.

James stopped what he was doing, frying pan held aloft and spoon balancing a chunk of egg. She looked drop-dead gorgeous. Yes, he'd seen her in a designer dress, tight jeans that made his stomach roll with longing, and cute beach outfits but dressed like that, how she was now, bloody hell, it almost beat her being naked.

"I'm sorry, I couldn't eat breakfast in my dress." She fiddled with the hem of the white shirt he'd worn the evening before. It hit her just below the line of her panties and she'd rolled the sleeves up to reveal her slim wrists and hands. The top few buttons were undone showing off her cleavage.

"I think…" He paused and swallowed. "That you should wear my clothes more often."

She laughed and took a seat at the island. "Not quite my style."

"I beg to differ." He resumed spooning out the eggs then added the bacon and sausages. "Here," he said, sliding a plate her way. "Eat up."

"It looks amazing." She licked her lips and picked up a

knife and fork. "Thank you."

"And tea, white no sugar, right?"

"You have a good memory."

"I do where you're concerned." He sat opposite her and started on his own breakfast.

"So are you on set again today?" Megan asked, spreading butter on her toast.

"Yes, full day of filming, we don't start till late morning, though. I like the sun high in the sky for this documentary. It works with the mood and what we're trying to get at."

She nodded and chewed on some bacon.

"Then we'll work till late. I've got lots to get through and the sooner the better. I'll confess I'm really not enjoying this project."

"I guessed as much. Not really your thing."

"Exactly. Plus Tate is only available for a set length of time then he's off to do his next movie."

"Oh yes, he's playing an English lord or something. That's how we got chatting, he wanted me to help him with his accent."

James shovelled in a pile of egg then munched on toast. He didn't want to talk about Tate over breakfast, his first breakfast with Megan. The guy was a prat, it was just a shame the rest of the world couldn't see that — instead they idolised him. "Perhaps we can go for dinner later, when I've wrapped up for the day?" he suggested, changing the subject.

"That would be nice, or you could come to ours? Brendon, Georgie and I will cook for you."

James raised his eyebrows.

"Yes, I want you to meet my friends." She laughed then reached for her tea. "Brendon and you will get on like a house on fire."

"I'm sure we will because I get the feeling he adores you, and anyone that has your best interests at heart is going to be a good guy in my book."

"He's great, a wonderful friend and a talent when it

137

comes to knowing what's hot and what's not and when and how to hit the market." She speared a chunk of sausage. "And Georgie is only here for another day or two then she's heading back to the UK. She has wedding plans to organise."

"Oh yes, of course." James remembered Megan telling him about the engagement—it was one of the first conversations they'd had. Something suddenly occurred to him. "So Georgie got engaged just after all that happened with you and Dylan, in the church?"

"Yes." She glanced at her plate. "I tried so hard to be happy for her that day but my life had just turned upside down."

He set his knife aside and covered her hand with his.

She looked back up at him. "It's okay, though, it was a change for the best, I don't doubt that for a second, but just because I was the...jilter...it doesn't mean it didn't affect me."

"How do you mean?"

"Well I felt terrible. I'd really hurt Dylan, and disappointed all my family and friends."

"Well I won't dispute that the groom likely felt horrendous, but your true friends, and the people who know and love you, were they disappointed?"

She appeared to think for a moment. "Well, I guess not. Mum and Dad just want me to be happy and do the best for myself, and Brendon and Georgie confessed that they'd never really liked him."

"And they'd never said anything, Brendon and Georgie?"

"Well no." She shrugged. "I guess they didn't think it would be polite."

He smiled and resumed eating. "I see."

"But," she said, "I've made them promise to always tell me in the future what they think of any men I introduce to them."

"Oh." He reached for his tea. "I should be on my best behaviour tonight then. I wouldn't want them warning you off me."

She reached over and pressed a soft kiss on his cheek. "Just be yourself. I know they're going to think you're perfect for me."

A small flush rose on her cheeks as she leaned back and carried on eating.

James smiled. He thought he was perfect for her too. "What time do you want me?"

"Whenever suits you?"

"We'll wrap about seven so by the time I've got home, showered and headed down to Venice it will be about eight."

"I'll look forward to it." She smiled.

It was a special smile that went straight to his soul. A smile he wanted to start and end each day with. A smile he'd dreamed about having here in LA with him.

Yep, life was good and he had a feeling it was just going to keep on getting better, just as soon as this damn documentary was out of the way and Tate Simmons was out of their lives forever.

The sun was relentless. Even the sea breeze didn't seem to be taking the edge off the blistering heat.

James adjusted his cap and wiped his fingers over his damp brow. The lifeguards were used to the heat and were coping admirably but Tate was driving him to distraction. He'd arrived on set late, been grumpy with a group of fans hanging around the trailer then had muttered through his first three takes.

James had ordered him to go and have a coffee and take some paracetamol then come back. The order hadn't gone down well but nevertheless Tate had done as instructed.

Now they were all hanging about waiting for him. They'd done as much as they could but needed him to narrate a piece about resuscitation. James hoped to hell he was sitting in there learning his lines and not snoring the day away.

"For crying out loud," he said, turning to Grant. "This is ridiculous."

Grant took a slug from a bottle of water. "Tell me about it." He dragged his forearm over his mouth. "Want me to go and get him?"

James glanced at his watch. "Yeah, you'd better. We'll be a whole day behind otherwise and I can't think of anything more depressing."

Grant tossed his bottle of water into the shade of the parasol that was keeping his equipment cool then stomped off towards the trailer.

James watched him go for a moment then set his attention on the beachfront homes that led the way to Venice Beach. The houses appeared small from where he was down by the shore front but still, the wide path in front of them — currently filled with boarders, skaters and dog walkers — led the way to Megan.

She'd said that she would be home all day. She and Brendon had a ton of emails to work through and phone calls to make and they'd had to set a day aside to do it. Then there were more launches, the possibility of billboard adverts for Winter Shoes, and an exciting lead that might give her a television appearance to shout about her product.

He smiled, despite his discomfort in the heat. She was such a sparky woman. She had an idea, a product, that she believed in and she was going for it. He admired that very much about her. Not to mention the product was pretty awesome. He'd seen enough of her designs to know that once the word got out here they'd be a hit.

He reached for his bottle of water and took a drink.

"Hey, boss, what's up?"

He turned. Tate was ambling towards him, shades in place and his creased shirt done up one button wrong.

"Ah good," James said. "You're here."

Tate huffed and rubbed his hand over his jaw. He had a sprinkle of blond stubble but instead of making him look rough it just enhanced his surfer dude look.

"Oh, Tate," one of the female lifeguards said. "You're all askew." She pointed to his shirt.

He glanced downward. "Ah, damn. Thanks, babe."

"Want me to do it?" She smiled and set her hand on her slim waist, cocking her hip to the right.

"Have at it," he said, returning her smile.

James held in a groan as she sidled up to him and made a show of fussing over his shirt. It was no doubt in that state because he'd been sleeping instead of learning his lines.

She did up the button then smoothed her hands over it.

"What's your name?" Tate asked.

"Jennifer." She didn't take her gaze from his face. "Jennifer Orla."

"What a pretty name."

"Thank you." She giggled.

"Give me a break," Grant muttered under his breath as he picked up his camera.

"Tell me about it," James agreed.

"Oh…" Grant said, freezing and staring at the security barrier they had around their filming area. "Looks like we have company."

James followed his line of sight. Emerging from the crowd and walking over the sand like some kind of goddess, was Megan.

Wearing a short pale pink dress and mules, along with a straw hat and a matching pink scarf, she looked good enough to eat.

She raised her hand in greeting when she spotted him looking her way.

"What's she doing here?" Grant asked.

"Come to see me." James threw him a look.

"But I thought…?" He nodded at Tate.

"Most definitely not." He scowled then started to walk towards her.

"Hi," she said when he was closer.

"Hi, yourself. Everything okay?"

141

"Yes, I realised that I hadn't given you our address." She held out a folded piece of paper. "So you can find us later." He smiled. "You could have text me."

She glanced at the floor then back up at him, cocked her head. "I wanted to see you. I know you're busy, so only for a second." She paused. "I'm sorry, you're busy. I'll go." She stepped away.

"No, it's fine." He was thrilled that she'd wanted to see him. In fact it had made his day.

"Hey, baby, what are you doing here?"

James felt as though knives had stabbed his ears. The sound of Tate's voice right next to his shoulder made his blood boil.

"Tate?" Megan looked at him in surprise. "I..."

"You've come to say you're sorry about last night. Don't sweat it. I got caught up too." He shrugged and went to reach for her. "Often the way at these events you end up getting split up."

Megan side-stepped out of his grasp.

Tate frowned, but only for a microsecond. "You want to go get some lunch? Maybe let the crowd see us *together* together this time. You caused quite a stir last night, mystery woman." He gave a lecherous wink.

What an idiot.

"Er, no, I'm...er busy..." Megan glanced at James.

She'd gone from being sunny and relaxed to uncomfortable and frosty.

And it is all Tate's fault.

"You're busy?" Tate repeated, disbelief lacing his tone.

"Yes, with Winter Shoes. Very busy today."

James clenched his fists. Busy. *Yes, she'll always be too busy for you, Tate.* Why couldn't he get that into his pretty head? As far as James was concerned, Tate could take a run and jump right into the middle of the damn ocean, and if no one ever saw him again all the better.

"Oh, blow that work off." Tate laughed. "I could use some hair of the dog, let's go out and get slammed, baby."

He banged his hand on James' shoulder. "Boss man knows he's not going to get much out of me today in this state, don't you, buddy?"

James twisted his torso and shook Tate off. If his blood had been boiling before it was so on fire now his veins were actually scorched. Plus it was as though burning red ants were crawling over his skin. His peripheral vision had a scarlet hue to it and was a little foggy.

Calm down.

"No," James said through gritted teeth.

"No what?" Tate held up his palms. "I can't go for lunch?"

"No, you're not going out with her." He paused. "Ever."

"Ever?" Tate slid his glasses to the tip of his nose and studied James with his piercing blue eyes. "Ahh, yes, you like her, don't you? There's history. Well I'm sorry, buddy, but you're just going to have to admit defeat on this one." He jerked his head towards Megan. "She picked me."

"You—" James felt his whole body tense. It was as if his muscles weren't his own.

"Mate." Grant's hand pressed on his shoulder, a steadying presence. "Come on, let's get to work," Grant said.

James pulled in a breath. The hot air did nothing to dampen his temper.

"This way," Grant went on, urging him to step away.

James glanced around him at the people observing the filming and the crew and lifeguards watching them talk. It seemed wherever Tate was there were adoring spectators.

"James," Grant said again.

James stepped away, keeping his attention on Megan.

"I'll see you later," she said, giving an understanding smile. "Okay?"

He nodded, not trusting himself to speak.

"Ah, babe, you're breaking my heart," Tate said, banging his hand on his chest and looking Megan up and down. "Don't go and leave me..." He chuckled, clearly enjoying the fact that he'd wound up his director to the point he was unable to form words. "Come to lunch."

Megan turned and took one step up the beach.

Quick as a flash, Tate reached out and set a playful slap on her arse. "Such a sexy booty," he said. "Bring that sexy booty out to lunch with me."

Megan gasped and spun to face him, shock on her face.

James heard a roar in his ears. His heart pounded against his ribs. Energy rushed through his core, to his shoulders, his arms, his fist.

His fist landed on Tate's jaw.

He was aware of the feel of skin and bone colliding with his knuckles. Of soft flesh yielding and bone not moving.

"What the...?" Tate clutched his jaw and glared at James. His sunglasses had gone flying to the sand as he'd staggered. "You asshole!" He pressed his palm to his jawline.

"No, you're the asshole. Megan is with me, get it?"

"I'm not taking this shit from you." Tate lunged forward, head down in a bulldozer move.

James felt the full force of Tate's head thrusting into his belly. The wind was knocked from him and he lurched backwards.

The sand was hard. He knocked his head on it but that didn't stop him. He drew up his knees, caught Tate between the legs and was rewarded with a guttural groan.

"James!" Megan's voice barely penetrated the roaring in his ears.

Suddenly Tate reared up.

James saw the fist flying towards him a nanosecond before it hit. His cheek hurt, as though it had imploded, pain radiated up to his eye, over his scalp and down his neck.

But the pain just added fuel to the fire of his rage. He pulled in air and threw his weight at Tate, tipping him over so he was the one on top. He drew back his fist, intent on landing another hit over the first so Tate would really have something to remember him by.

A steely grip landed around his forearm then another around his waist. James was aware of being hauled backwards, his heels dragging on the sand. He fought his binds, the hands that held him, desperate to get back to Tate and finish what he'd started.

"Get off me."

No one on the planet got away with slapping his woman on the arse. Hollywood A-lister or not.

"Jesus Christ, man, what are you doing?" Grant said.

"Get the hell off me."

"No."

James tried to shake free and glared at Tate. He was being held back by two of the larger lifeguards and looked as keen to finish off what had been started as James was.

"Stay away from her," James shouted.

"Fuck you!" Tate stilled and stood tall. He looked at the men next to him. "Get off me, we've got one hell of a fucking audience."

Is that all he's thinking about?

"You gonna calm down?" Grant asked.

"Yeah." He didn't feel calm.

"Promise."

"Yes!" He shifted his shoulders and found himself released. He spun around, searching for Megan.

Where is she?

Panic darted through him. Where was she? Was she okay?

"She's gone." Grant nodded in the direction of the crowd. "Just saw her disappear through there."

"Shit. I had better go—"

"No." Again Grant gripped his upper arm. "She looked pretty shocked. I'd give her a few hours if I were you."

James looked at him. "Why?"

"Well you went a bit insane for a bit there. Not a good look." He shrugged. "Chicks don't like that."

"But he…"

"I know. I saw. He's a prize idiot who doesn't know his boundaries because he's always been worshipped but come on…you just messed up a ten-million-dollar jawline."

James shut his eyes. *Shit.* Grant was right. Tate wasn't

your average guy in a club that might cope with a bit of a battering—not that James was in the habit of fighting by any stretch of the imagination—but a man whose face was idolized by an army of fans and relied upon to bring in the big bucks.

His anger faded as fast as it had arrived. What a fool he'd been. Now he'd upset Megan and risked his reputation and possibly his relationship with the studio.

He frowned at Tate, who was inspecting his shades and allowing one of the lifeguards to brush the sand from his back. The pretty young girl, Jennifer, who'd flirted with him earlier was making soothing noises and studying his jaw, which already had an angry red bruise on it.

"You okay?" Grant peered at him.

"Yeah." Apart from the fact he didn't have a time machine, and the bone beneath his right eye felt as though it had its own pulse and was sending pain shooting over his skull, then yeah, he was hunky-bloody-dory.

"Hey, Tate," Grant called, putting himself between James and Tate. "Why don't you go get makeup to work their magic on you? Go get cleaned up and we might actually be able to get some work done."

Tate threw a scathing look at Grant that he then passed on to James.

The hairs on the back of James' neck bristled.

"Yeah," Tate said, shaking his head. "I'll do that, as long as you keep that bat-shit-crazy director of yours out of my way.

"We still have to work together," James said, trying to add a modicum of maturity to his voice.

"Not for long, thank God." Tate went to walk past him. When level, he drew close. "You do realize the entire world is going to see you attacking me. They"—he nodded at the crowd—"will have filmed the entire episode. Then, when she, Megan, sees how you turned into an animal and attacked, me, who do you think she'll want to be with?"

"Yeah, but you'll still be an asshole." James clenched his

fists. "Because I'm more than just a pretty face."

"Ah yes..." Tate rubbed the increasing swelling on his cheek. "Will be interesting to see what the lawyers say about that, won't it?"

"Why don't you just take it like a man...?" James could feel the heat rising in him again, his focus fudging.

"Get out of here." Grant jerked his thumb towards the trailer. "Now."

Tate rolled his eyes then ambled away. He threw a wave at the crowd and grinned.

"Dickhead," James mumbled.

"Dickhead who's just got you into a whole heap of trouble with everyone." Grant sighed. "And all over a woman. I always knew that one had got under your skin."

James turned to him. He opened his mouth to argue but then shut it again because there was no denying it. Megan was under his skin, in his dreams and in his heart.

He just hoped he hadn't messed it up with her beyond repair.

12

Megan raced from the scene of violence and carnage. She couldn't believe what had happened on the beach set.

One second she'd been removing herself from a very uncomfortable conversation between her, James and Tate, then she'd felt a slap on her behind and all hell had broken out.

She rushed along the path, eager to get away from the excited crowd.

The sight of James hurling a punch at Tate played over and over in her mind. The way Tate's head and neck had snapped sideways from the impact had made her feel instantly sick. Then Tate had lunged for James, she'd seen pain on James' face as the air had been bashed from his lungs and he'd hit the sand.

After that she hadn't hung around.

She'd left them to it.

She didn't want to see anymore.

If they wanted to behave like primary school kids arguing over who was going to play with the train track then she'd leave them to it. What kind of men did that?

Her heart was racing, her breaths coming quick. She dodged a woman with three handbag dogs on sparkling leads. The sooner she was back with Brendon and Georgie, the better. She needed them, her firm, solid friends. The people who she knew inside and out.

She'd thought she'd known James but his temper had flared in an instant.

She'd thought she'd known Dylan but his love for her had been destructive.

Tears welled in her eyes as she turned to the row of houses her new home was set in. She couldn't compare them, really she couldn't. James was nothing like Dylan, he was sweet and caring and he admired and respected her.

Didn't he?

Again, the sight of him thumping Tate filled her mind's eye.

Hurriedly she jogged up the path and shoved the key in the lock.

"Is that you back already?" Georgie called out from the kitchen. "I thought you'd hang out for a bit with lover boy?"

Megan flung the keys onto the hall table.

She looked up.

Brendon stood in the kitchen doorway with a mug of coffee in his hand. His face was one of alarm.

"Oh dear Lord," he said. "What the blithering hell has happened now?"

Megan stared at him for a moment then the tears spilled over. A sob burst up from her chest and rattled her ribs.

"Megan."

"Sweetpea."

She was aware of both her friends' arms around her. Holding her close, they made soothing noises. Georgie stroked her hair and Brendon rubbed a circle over her back.

Their sympathy just made the sobs come all the harder and the tears flow all the faster.

"We need wine," Brendon said, steering them all towards the kitchen. "I know it's not wine o'clock and we still have work to do, but this is clearly an emergency."

"What's happened?" Georgie said. "Please tell us. Has there been an accident?"

The real fear in Georgie's voice pulled Megan up. "No," she said, wiping the moisture from beneath her eyes. "No, not an accident...just a...fight."

"A fight?" Brendon's eyes widened. "Who, what, why, where, when?"

"On the beach." Megan sat on the bar stool Georgie had directed her to and ripped off a piece of kitchen roll to blot her cheeks with.

"On the beach?" Brendon pulled open the fridge then retrieved a bottle of sauvignon blanc.

Megan nodded and sniffed.

"What are you talking about?" Georgie sent her gaze roaming over Megan. "Not you, you're not hurt, are you? Did someone attack you?"

"No, not me, I'm fine." She paused and watched Brendon pour three huge glasses of wine. "It was between James and Tate."

Brendon gasped and stared at her. "No freakin' way?"

She nodded, the awful scene flashing before her again. "Yes, freakin' way."

"Well isn't this just the most *Gone with the Wind, Doctor Zhivago, Rocky* and *Love, Actually* romance there has ever been?" He set down the wine bottle and clasped his hands beneath his chin.

"It's not supposed to be entertainment," Megan said, frowning. "This is my life."

"I know," Georgie said soothingly, handing out the wine. "But you've got to admit you're either flying high or swinging low right now. This morning we could hardly peel you off the ceiling when you came in, and now, well…" She shrugged. "It's the end of the world."

"Darling, darling, it is not the end of the world." Brendon held up his hands. "You have two men, two hot, successful, drop-dead gorgeous men fighting over you, it doesn't get any better!"

"I think it does." Megan took a big slug of wine.

"No, no it doesn't." Brendon placed his hands on his hips. "If I had two dreamboat guys throwing fists over me, I'd be in bloody heaven."

"But it was awful." Megan shook her head.

"Start at the beginning," Georgie said, tipping her head encouragingly.

Megan pulled in a deep breath. "Well I went to see James, as you know, just to confirm him coming here for dinner later, make sure he knew where we were." She paused then clasped her hand over her mouth.

"What?" Brendon asked.

"He can't come here. Well he can, but we'll have to go out."

"No we won't," Brendon said firmly.

Tears welled in Megan's eyes again. She didn't want to see James. She didn't want him on the doorstep. Not tonight. She needed some time to filter through her thoughts.

"If that's what you want, Megan." Georgie rubbed her back. "Carry on."

Megan sniffed. "Well I was just talking to him, telling him I'd see him for dinner and Tate came over." She paused. "You know what he's like, full of bravado and the big I am."

"Everything you tell me about him puts me off." Georgie pulled a face.

"It should." Megan had another drink, willing the wine to take the sting from the last half an hour. "Anyway, he started going on about us going for lunch, about the fact that I'd been with him at the ceremony and I was his mystery woman. I knew it was winding James up, I could see his cheeks going red and his lips doing this flat line thing, as if he daren't speak for what he might say."

"Bloody hell." Brendon took a seat, clearly loving the drama and soaking in every word

"He wanted me to go for lunch with him, let the crowd know we were an item and then..." Megan said.

"What?" Georgie asked. "Then what."

"Well I said no, that I was busy and turned to go. It was then I..." She shut her eyes. "Felt a slap on my arse."

"No way?" Brendon said. "Who?"

"Who do you think?" Megan looked between her two friends.

"Tate," they said in unison.

"Yes."

They both gasped.

"He just went and slapped my behind and told me to bring my sexy booty out to lunch with him."

"He didn't?" Georgie exclaimed.

Megan nodded.

"Well fuck a duck," Brendon said. "Would you ever believe it?"

"You'd better believe it," Megan said. "Well James certainly did, because next thing I knew he'd thumped Tate square in the jaw."

"Oh my God, no, he didn't mark that beautiful face?" Brendon clasped his hands over his cheeks.

"I'm sure he did but I didn't hang around to find out. Tate's a big bloke, works out, he turned on James and next thing they were rolling on the sand about to beat each other to a pulp." Megan bit on her bottom lip. "I just got the hell out of there. I pushed through the crowds and got back here as fast as I could."

"It'll be all over YouTube." Georgie shoved her hand through her hair.

"Why?" Megan asked.

"Well there's bound to be someone in the crowd who had a phone and videoed it."

"Oh no..." Megan sighed. "Well thank goodness I didn't hang around."

"You did the right thing coming home," Brendon said. "Don't know how you did it, I wouldn't have been able to resist staying to find out who won."

"There's no winners." Megan drained her wine. "Just losers because right now the only thing I know for sure is I don't want either of them." She stood from the stool. Her knees still felt a little weak but the wine had soothed her nerves. "Let's go out."

"What?" Georgie asked. "But we've still..."

"Got things to do. I know. I just don't want to be here if... *when* James turns up."

"Well if that's how you feel—" Brendon also polished off his wine. "I'd say this calls for some superior cocktails. Let's hit the Moonbar—we promised Georgie we'd take her there and we're running out of time before she gets on her jet plane and hightails it back to Blighty."

"Excellent idea." Georgie's face lit up. "I can call Tom from there too."

Megan reached for her friend's hand. "Have you spoken to him yet today?"

"Yes, as soon as I woke up, it was his mid-afternoon, but I said I'd call again later."

"You'll be glad to get home and see him."

"Yes, but sad to leave here."

"And we'll be sad to see you go, but no sadness yet." Brendon clapped his hands. "Come on, peeps, we need some glamour and some sparkle. We're off to the hippest place in town."

Two hours later Megan sat with Brendon and Georgie in the famous Moonbar. It was an open-air, ivy-covered pavilion that overlooked a pool and had views to die for over the city and out to the Pacific. The chunky furniture was cream leather, the tables held fresh flowers and candles and a small crowd of beautiful people hung about drinking cocktails.

Megan brushed a crumb from the electric blue dress she'd pulled on for the occasion. She'd teamed it with elegant silver heels and a long slim necklace that wrapped around her neck several times.

She clinked glasses with Georgie, who looked amazing in a white mini skirt and backless black vest. With her blonde hair piled high and a tan, she was in perfect holiday mode.

Brendon looked handsome too in a flowery pink shirt and neon green trousers. He had on new pink shoes that were slim and pointy, making his feet appear huge next to his skinny ankles.

"To cocktails with friends, flights of fancy and fights on the beach," Brendon said. "You can't say it's been a boring holiday, Georgie."

She smiled. "It's always fun with you two."

"Sorry we've been a bit waylaid with Winter Shoe business," Megan said.

"Oh, it's only been a few days and it was fun to be part of the excitement, besides, this makes up for it all." She nodded at the view. "It's amazing."

The usual smog hung over suburbia but out to sea, the sky was crystal clear and a dense blue. "It's amazing."

"So," Brendon said, "dare we look at YouTube?" He held up his iPhone.

"No!" Megan said.

"Spoilsport." He frowned.

"Let's not *spoil* the moment," Megan said. "Tate and James are not worth it." Even as she spoke her heart sank. James was worth it. He was worth everything and more, yet to see him strike out...it had scared her.

Brendon sighed dramatically. "Okay..."

"I'd just rather not...for now."

There was a burst of laughter and a few cheers from the clubhouse.

Megan glanced over and saw the white drapes that led to the bar area fluttering in the breeze. They reminded her of the ones James had in his home, the ones she'd stared at that very morning after she'd woken as she'd heard James moving around the kitchen.

Damn.

She'd never in a million years have guessed the events of the day. She'd thoroughly expected to be with James right now, enjoying seeing him interact with her friends, watching Brendon flirt shamelessly and observing how Georgie would grill him.

More voices drifted from the clubhouse.

Megan sat back and sipped on her drink and watched as a new group of glamorous LA beauties wandered to the pool area. They were a mixture of men and women—the women in tight dresses, the men in sharp trousers and neat shirts. All could have been models or actors, not a flaw between them.

They headed their way, making for the spare seats with equally awesome views not far behind where they sat.

A man, tall and slim with a black shirt and neat black hair, stared at her as they approached.

Megan looked away.

She'd had enough of men to last her a few years at least.

Still she could feel his gaze on her.

She glanced back at him.

He was poking his friend. "Look. It's her...from the beach brawl."

Megan's heart rate picked up.

Surely she hadn't heard that right.

The friend stared at her too before a flash of recognition crossed over his face. "Oh yes. So it is."

They came to a stop, still staring. The rest of the crowd did the same.

"You got a problem?" Georgie said to the guy in the black shirt.

"Ah, ah, not us, but you, baby" — he pointed at Megan — "are all over the news. Just seen your pretty face on the TV in there." He jabbed his thumb in the direction of the indoor bar. "Seems Tate Simmons is willing to fight for you."

"Lucky bitch," a girl in a silver spray-on dress said. She then laughed, a high-pitched, nasty cackle.

"What's your name?" the guy asked again.

"None of your beeswax," Brendon said.

Megan could barely believe what she was hearing. She was on the news? The *fight* was on the news? She thought it would hit YouTube for sure but the actual news? Was it that interesting to the world?

"Well, I think you'll find that the world is gonna make it their business to find out who you are, sugar," another man said. "Because you showed up to an event on the arm of one of Hollywood's hottest men then he fights to make you his, well..." He paused and shook his head. "That is the stuff of Hollywood drama and everyone is goin' to wanna piece of you."

"I— Can you just…" She pressed her fingers to her temple. "Leave us alone, please."

"Yeah, sure. We have our own stories to tell, but good luck with yours."

They moved away in a series of clacking heels and giggles.

"Oh my God," Brendon said, "you're on the news? This could be awesome publicity if we play it right."

"I don't know. It's not the kind of exposure I wanted for Winter Shoes."

"What, one of Hollywood's hottest stars and an award-winning director fighting over *you*? Baby, it doesn't get much better. Like he just said, everyone wants to know your name." He paused and pressed his hand over his chest. "And have you any idea how much it killed me not to tell them your name? Instinct said hand out your business cards, invite the beautiful people to LA Hype for a personal shopping experience."

"Yeah, they look like they have money," Georgie said. "Likely all sons and daughters of the city's super-rich."

"Well thank you, Brendon, for not revealing it. We need to decide how to handle this."

"Yes, but first we need to know what we're dealing with." Brendon pulled out his phone. "I think you'll agree it's time to look."

"Okay."

He scrawled for a few seconds then angled the phone so they could all see the screen.

A national live news channel popped up, the male reader looking stiff and serious.

"Tate Simmons fans have been shocked this afternoon to see him involved in real life drama, and not his usual high-octane but carefully scripted scenes. While filming a documentary in Santa Monica, a brawl broke out, seemingly over a woman."

The screen flipped to a slightly shaky video taken from behind where James had stood. It showed her talking to the two men then turning to walk away. Her face was in clear view and the breeze flattening her clothes to her body. As she turned, Tate reached out to slap her bum.

"Honestly!" Georgie said.

"Classy," Brendon muttered.

Megan watched in horror as for the second time she saw James strike out. The two men became the centre of the screen, the person recording the event having zoomed in. Within seconds, they were tumbling on the floor, scrabbling and groaning, sand pluming around them. She saw James screw up his face as a punch landed on his cheek.

She gasped and pressed her hands to her own cheeks.

On and on it went. Their bodies seemed to be a wild mass of limbs. Suddenly James was on top, his fist drawn back, his hair messy and his polo-shirt creased and yanked sideways around the collar.

"*Fans watched on in horror,*" the newsreader continued, "*as well-respected LA director James Carter swung for the star, catching him on his jaw. Both men landed punches in what's been described as a hot-tempered, love-induced brawl, before being pulled apart by cast and crew.*"

The screen withdrew, showing that Megan was no longer there. Both men were glaring at each other as Grant and lifeguards held them apart.

"*So the big question is…*" the newsreader said as the screen filled with his face again. "*Who is the mystery girl? The speculation started last night when Tate arrived at The Sparkling Stars Awards with her on his arm.*"

A picture of Megan and Tate looking cosy flashed up on the screen — the pose when he'd touched his head to hers and held her as if they were lovers.

"*They appeared to be very much in love and he hinted that he couldn't have got to where he is without her in his acceptance speech after winning best actor.*"

"I still can't believe he didn't let you have a moment of glory on the red carpet and introduce you. So damn mean," Brendon muttered.

"Shh," Georgie said.

"I was only there as his arm candy," Megan said.

The newsreader frowned, pressed his index finger to his ear for a moment then looked back at the camera. *"Word is just in that we have a name for the mystery woman."* He sounded excited.

"Here we go," Brendon said.

A picture of Megan flashed up on screen. It was a professional photograph she'd had taken a few months ago for her website. She wore a white silk blouse, skinny jeans and trademark white heels studded with jewels. She was smiling and her head was tipped slightly so her hair tumbled over her right shoulder.

"British-born Megan Winter is the woman behind Winter Shoes that is, apparently, taking A-list shoppers on Rodeo Drive by storm. At just thirty years old, she's not just a pretty face, but has also made a name for herself on UK television advising the nation on stylish footwear."

"And there we have it," Brendon said, rubbing his hands together. "The national spotlight money just couldn't buy." He sounded incredibly pleased with himself.

"Shh!" Georgie and Megan said together.

"And it seems her style and smile have stolen the heart of Tate Simmons, so all the ladies out there who were hoping to bag him will be crying into their pillows tonight. This man is so in love he's willing to fight for his woman. I can almost hear wedding bells." He paused. *"Now here's Graham with the weather."*

The screen flashed to a picture of the American map with swirls and numbers all over it.

"Oh my giddy heart." Brendon pressed the phone face down on his leg, silencing a spiel about a threatening storm on the East Coast. "Would you ever...?"

'True love? Me and Tate?" Megan held out her palms. "Didn't anyone see that for what it was? I was walking away from him, he slapped me on the behind, James hit him first, he was only retaliating..."

"People draw their own conclusions, and it seems they want to conclude that you and Tate are an item and he was fighting for you. It makes for a good story and this place is all about the story, be it real or not."

"You did look pretty cosy on that picture from the ceremony," Georgie said, sipping her drink and waggling her eyebrows.

"It was all contrived by him." Megan shook her head. "Immediately after it was taken the reporters were asking for my name. I'd have happily given it then chatted for a moment but he pulled me away. It was all Tate, Tate, Tate."

"So why did he?" Georgie directed her gaze at Megan's bum. "Slap you?"

"A show of possession?" Brendon said. "He knows James likes our Megan and let's just say..." He pressed his lips together.

"What?" Georgie asked.

"They don't get on," Megan said. "Or that was the impression I got. I don't think it's just because of me, there's more to it. James really didn't want to do Tate's documentary."

"More than an impression," Georgie said. "They looked out for blood."

"Or certainly our hero James did," Brendon said. "Clearly he didn't take kindly to someone touching the woman he'd had in his bed the night before."

"Bloody hell..." Megan moaned. "This is such a mess. Not only is my relationship with James screwed, now everyone thinks Tate and I are heading for the chapel."

"I don't think your relationship with James is screwed," Georgie said with a shrug.

"But...?"

"He was defending your honour."

"It's actually quite romantic," Brendon added. "Real knight in shining armour stuff."

Megan felt a tap on her shoulder. She turned and saw the man in the black shirt who'd spotted her earlier.

"Megan Winter," he said. "Seems your face *and* name have hit the headlines." He held out a pen and a piece of paper. "Can I have your autograph?"

"Well, I really—" Megan stared at the pen. Why would anyone want her autograph?

"Of course." Brendon took it and pressed it into her hand. "What's your name?"

"Mark."

"To Mark with love." Brendon tapped the paper. "Chop chop."

Megan did as instructed. It was all happening so quickly.

"Thanks," the guy said as she handed it back. "I guess I'll need another one when you become Megan Simmons." He smiled. "Do you come here often?"

"Not really…"

"We're just slumming it tonight," Brendon said with a laugh. "But nice to meet you." He kind of flicked his fingers as if shooing the man away.

The guy gave Megan a lingering look then wandered off.

"That was weird," Megan said.

"Get used to it. You're famous, it's what you wanted, remember?"

"I wanted to be famous for my designs, not having men fight like dogs over me."

"Well, I guess that's the nature of the game." Brendon drained his cocktail and stood. "You don't always get to choose what gets you in the spotlight."

"Are we going?" Georgie asked, casting a wistful look over the city's darkening skyline.

"Yes, come on. We're going to need our beauty sleep. I get the feeling tomorrow is going to be a whirlwind of PR activity."

As he'd spoken, his phone rang.

"Hello." He pressed it to his ear and examined his nails. "Yes, this is Megan Winter's Public Relations office."

Megan gripped her glass and wondered if the tumbling feeling in her stomach would ever reduce.

"Ah yes, that sounds like something she'd be very interested in. I haven't got her diary with me, and obviously

160

I would need to check with my client. Can I give you a call back tomorrow?" He paused. "Okay, thank you. Yes."

He re-locked his phone.

"Who was that?" Georgie asked.

"The *Paul Piper* show, they want Megan on their couch this Friday evening." He shook his head. "Doesn't get much better than that!"

"Oh blimey…" Megan said. Could she really go on a chat show and talk about all of this? She didn't even have it straight in her own head. What would she say? How would she explain any of it? She'd been on live TV and talked shoes and fashion, she could do that, but her relationship…?

"And before you say you can't do it, of course you can, and if you don't then I'm resigning." Brendon waggled his finger at her. "This is too good an opportunity to miss, and what's more, it's free."

Georgie wrapped her arm around Megan's shoulder and pulled her close. "It will all be fine, and it won't seem nearly so bad in the morning. Come on, you look worn out. Let's get you home to bed."

"I think that might be a good idea."

As they all stood, Brendon's phone rang again. He answered it. "Winter Shoes PR." He held up his finger. "No comment." He shut the phone.

"What?" Megan asked.

"Paps," he said, rolling his eyes. "Wanting to know when you and Tate are getting married."

"You should have put them straight. Nothing on this earth would make me want to marry that egotistical, misogynistic, vain…" Megan felt her temper simmer.

"Shh." Brendon tapped his lips and glanced around. "Let everyone keep guessing until the *Paul Piper* show. It will build up the speculation and then be a wow moment when you say it's all off." He giggled. "You've gone up in the world from jilting Dylan Dunkin-Buckshaw, that's for certain. Now you're going for humiliating one of the most famous actors on the West Coast of America."

13

They hopped in a cab outside the Moonbar. Megan sat in the middle, feeling cocooned and safe with her friends' shoulders touching hers. But still she gripped her purse, and her stomach had a tight feeling, like a ball of elastic bands that was knotted and likely to start bouncing around at any moment.

She glanced at the back of the cab driver's head and hoped he wouldn't recognise her as Tate's mystery woman. It wasn't what she wanted to be known as. She'd been happy to be his date, would have been happier if he'd introduced her to the LA media, but his woman, his rock, his bride-to-be, that just wasn't on.

Her heart beat fast as they navigated through the traffic. She pictured James standing before her on the beach the night before. He'd looked so handsome in his tuxedo and with the breeze ruffling his hair. She'd had an urge to just fall into his arms, go to that place where nothing else mattered as long as they were together.

Which is exactly what they'd done.

She craved the chance to go there again now. Feel his arms around her, his lips on hers and his body close. She shut her eyes and inhaled. His remembered scent filled her nose and she swept her tongue over her lips, recalling his flavour.

But what was the point? It was all over now. *They* were all over now.

She felt a well of tears emerging and blinked, hoping they wouldn't overspill.

Brendon's phone rang again.

"Now who is it?" he said exasperatedly. "If it's those damn paps again..." He looked at the screen. "Oh, it's Zane." His voice softened.

Megan looked at him—a smile had spread on his face.

"Hey, you, how's it hanging?" He paused then laughed at the response.

Megan and Georgie rolled their eyes at each other. Megan was pleased that her tears appeared to have been reabsorbed. But still, she couldn't shake the cracked feeling in her chest, it was if a lump of lead had settled there and was splitting in two.

"Yes, yes, I know. She is spectacular, couldn't have gone better." Brendon giggled. "That's what I said, no publicity is bad publicity. We'll take it all and then some."

He pressed his hand on Megan's leg as if reassuring her that his words weren't to be taken too seriously.

"What, now?" he said, surprise in his voice. "Well..." He glanced at his watch. "Okay, that sounds like an excellent plan. I'll see you soon."

He tapped his phone and dropped it into his shirt pocket.

"Going somewhere?" Georgie asked.

"Why yes." He grinned. "The delectable Zane has invited me for a late bite to eat, I'm meeting him at O'Connell's Bar in twenty."

"That's nice," Megan said. She took his hand and gave it a squeeze. At least someone's love life in LA was going well. "And make sure you relax. You've been going hell for leather on Winter Shoes lately and if your predictions are right, it will continue into tomorrow and beyond."

"Oh, don't you worry I'll relax all right." He smoothed his hand over his hair then straightened his collar. "Though Winter Shoes is likely to dominate the conversation for a while at least. Zane is over the moon that he found you first. This is great for LA Hype and he knows it. Expect to see your face in the shop window tomorrow, and on more press releases."

Megan gulped. She guessed she'd have to get used to seeing her face all over town for the next week or two at least. Then maybe she'd still be around but as the designer of Winter Shoes instead of the so-called bride-to-be of Tate

Simmons.

"This is us," Georgie said, leaning forward and indicating for the driver to pull over.

The car drew to a halt.

"I'll stay in," Brendon said. "Head straight on and see Zane. Will you girls be okay?"

"Of course," Megan said, "It's only a few minute walk from here."

"And we're tough, you know." Georgie grinned and passed Brendon a couple of notes for the fare. "Here, take this."

"Cheers," Brendon said. "Don't wait up."

Georgie laughed.

"We won't," Megan said.

The girls alighted from the cab. The area was well lit and Megan didn't feel worried about the short walk alongside the canal to their home.

Georgie linked arms with her. "Are you really not prepared to give James another chance?"

She sighed. "It was like I didn't know him back there on the beach and I thought I did." She looked down at her feet as they walked, admiring the way her shoes sparkled even in the dim light. For a moment it took her mind off the nightmare situation that was her love life but, of course, only for a moment. "I thought I knew Dylan too but it turned out I didn't. Who would have thought that he'd turn into the stalker from hell? That he'd try and force himself on me, be so deluded that he'd presumed I'd happily slip on another ring and go back to him."

"He certainly was deluded." Georgie tutted. "Look, I don't know James at all, but from what I've heard from you and Brendon, he's the opposite of Dylan. He's mature and grounded, well-respected and hard working. Plus he certainly sounds like he's into you for you and not just arm-candy or a bit of fun between the sheets."

Oh, but it is fun between the sheets.

Megan rid her mind of the image of James the night

before, looking glorious and seductive and making her the sole focus of his attention. A shiver wended its way up her spine and she caught her breath, the cooler night air catching in her throat.

Georgie turned to her. "See you can't, can you? You can't just brush him away. He's got to you, hasn't he?"

Megan pressed her lips together. Her heart and head were at war. She still felt bruised from the whole Dylan fiasco. Was she ready to take the plunge with more unknown? When James had been steadfast and consistent it hadn't been as scary, but that fight... It had left her reeling, if not physically then certainly emotionally.

Their house came into view but they continued to amble and were in no particular rush.

As they drew level with a bench, Georgie's phone rang. "Oh, I bet that's Tom. I haven't spoken to him since this afternoon."

Megan smiled. It seemed they couldn't go more than a few hours without connecting. Much as she knew Georgie was having a great time in LA, Megan also knew that her best friend would feel complete again once she arrived back in London and back into her fiancé's arms.

She wanted that kind of love—the elusive brand of desperate need that compelled a couple to be together.

James.

Just the thought of him made her heart flutter.

She wanted to be with him.

Could they have ever had the soul-deep, life-long love that Georgie and Tom had?

She guessed she'd never know.

"I'm going to sit out here," Georgie said, "and catch up with him." She put the phone to her ear and smiled. "Hey, sexy."

Megan gave her the thumbs-up and as she walked to the house pulled her keys from her purse. The sound of her heels echoed around the buildings and over the canal to her right. Reeds and lilies lined the way, shrouding the white picket fence that cordoned it off from children and dogs. Shadows rippled on the surface of the water, lit by the full moon.

She batted at a bug that landed on her arm and headed up the garden path. She let herself in but as she went to shut the door, something stopped it.

Not something — someone.

What the...?

A big black boot was shoved between the jamb and the door.

"Hey!" she said, ramming it harder, her heart galloping. Adrenaline raced into her system. Her stomach did a triple flip.

She threw her weight against the door, panic adding to the fear now.

"Ouch. Megan, for crying out loud."

James?

"Is that you...?" she managed, easing off from her frantic shoving. Had she really just heard James' voice?

"Please, let me in. I just want to talk to you."

Yes, she had. She stepped away and the door opened fully.

James stood on her step with a frown on his face, rubbing his hand.

"Ever heard of phones?" she snapped. "Or knocking?"

"I didn't think you'd answer my call so I decided to come round." He paused. "As we'd planned."

"Well I didn't want to see you, which was why I wasn't here."

His frown deepened. "Maybe that's why I didn't knock."

Even in the shadows she could see the bruise and swelling on his cheekbone, evidence that Tate had managed to land a decent right hook.

"How long have you been hanging about out there?"

"A few hours." He stepped in and shut the door.

Silence wrapped around them and the hall darkened.

She reached out and flicked on a table lamp, spreading an

amber glow over the wooden floor and up the walls.

They stared at each other.

Megan felt as though he was seeing right into her soul. Damn, she wanted him but...

She turned away. He was too much of a temptation. One more second looking at him, smelling his cologne, thinking of being in his arms and she would hurl herself at him.

"No." He grabbed her arm then spun her to face him.

"James..." She gasped.

"Don't walk away. Not again." He pulled her close.

She pressed her hands to his chest and shoved. "You shouldn't have come here."

He allowed her to push him away but then instantly stepped closer again.

Megan backed up until her shoulders hit the wall. He was so big, so dark looming over her and yet so damn handsome. "Please...leave..." She needed to be alone to sort through her feelings for him, build up an armour so she wouldn't succumb to temptation. "Now."

"Not a chance." He pressed his hands to the wall, palms flat on either side of her head, and lowered his face. He was breathing fast, and a determined glint flashed in his eyes.

She went to move.

But didn't.

She couldn't.

He'd trapped her and was looking at her in a way that made her think he'd never let her go.

I don't want him to ever let me go.

She shook her head and clenched her fists.

She wanted to reach for him, clutch his top and pull him closer until she could feel his chest against hers, their hearts beating as one. She wanted to crawl under his skin, become him, have him become her so there was nothing between them.

"James," she whispered. "No."

"If you said no like you actually meant it then maybe I'd leave," he said quietly. "I don't want to scare you or... I just want..."

She watched his mouth as he spoke, remembering how it felt when he kissed her.

"What, what do you want?" she managed.

Nothing.

"Why are you here?" She flexed her fingers then balled them into her palms again.

"Why do you think?"

She half shrugged.

"I'm here for you. I thought we'd got ourselves straight. That we were together." He paused, and a line formed between his eyebrows.

"James—" She glanced away. "I don't know, it's just..."

"What? Tell me. I'm no good at this guessing game."

His sharp tone riled her temper. "Okay, I'll tell you. On the beach today..."

"What about it?"

"You. You and Tate."

He clenched his jaw and a tendon twitched in his cheek, beneath the swelling. "Go on."

"It scared me. Seeing you and him like that."

"Me or him?"

"You. Seeing you hit him."

"Men sometimes hit each other."

She glanced away. He'd said it so matter-of-factly, as if it were common knowledge, acceptable.

"But never without reason, Megan." He reached for her chin and turned her back to face him. "And today there was a reason. A very good one."

"Well you'd better explain what possible reason can excuse violence."

"You."

"No, I don't want to be the cause of it." She tried to move away again. "Don't use me as a way of condoning a fight."

He didn't move.

She stayed trapped between him and the wall.

"Megan," he said, his voice softer. "Last night you were

warm and naked in my bed, this morning you were at breakfast with me wearing my shirt, *my* shirt, then within hours I saw that...that prat acting like you were his, slapping your arse for crying out loud." His voice had risen as he'd spoken. "So forgive me for wanting to pummel him, but he treated you with a disrespect that I just couldn't hack."

Megan stared at him and studied the earnest look in his eyes.

"And for the record," he said, his lips almost brushing hers, "I would do it again."

"James." She pushed him and he pulled back a couple of inches. "What kind of apology is that?"

"It isn't one." He cocked his head. "Well, I'm sorry for upsetting you, which I clearly have, but not for teaching that upstart a lesson."

"You should go." She didn't want him to but...

"No. Not until you understand that when a man loves a woman and another guy mistreats her then there are always consequences. What kind of bloke would I be if I'd let him get away with it? Get away with doing that to you."

She felt a small sob in her chest, bubbling to try to get to the surface. He loved her. He'd told her last night he did. The word had stayed with her all day. "James."

"Shh..." he said, stroking his finger down her cheek. "Please don't be upset anymore. We can put this behind us."

"But...Tate?" Her skin tingled where he touched her, small, luscious shivers running over her scalp and down her neck.

He lowered his voice until it was almost a growl. "Is nothing to do with us."

"Well *I* know that." God what a mess it was, though. She reached out and rested her hands on his chest, felt the heat of his skin pouring through the material of his top. "But the trouble is..."

"What?" He slipped a hand behind her, onto the small of her back and pulled her close. Their chests connected.

"The rest of the world seems to think we're an item." She thought of the headlines and the speculation in the tattle magazines. She was well and truly linked to Tate whether she wanted to be or not, and the only man she wanted to be linked to held her in his arms.

"You think I care about that?" He set a gentle kiss on her forehead.

Megan shut her eyes the moment that his lips connected with her.

"The rest of the world can go to hell," he whispered. "I'm only interested in what you think, what you know, and as long as he stays away from you that's the end of the matter, as far as I'm concerned."

"Even if I have to go on the *Paul Piper* show on Friday and field off questions about him?"

"Well I presume you'll be putting them straight about the *off* part of your brief acquaintance with Tate Simmons."

"Yes, of course…absolutely. We're no more." Megan bit her bottom lip. "And we didn't…you know."

"That's your business." He pulled his eyebrows together, again creating that line between them.

But she wanted him to know. It felt important to her. "I mean, he kissed me, once, you should know that but we never — "

He pressed his finger to her lips. "Don't talk of it, don't think of it." He lowered his head and removed his finger. "This is the only kiss you should think of from now on."

He captured her mouth in a soft, sensual kiss. His lips pressed to hers and his tongue peeked out to stroke hers.

Megan balled his top into her hands and melted against him. They were so right together. How could she have ever doubted it?

She pulled back a fraction. "James?"

"Mmm…" He stroked his hand over her hair, tucking a strand behind her ear.

"I'm sorry."

"You have nothing to be sorry for."

"I should have been here when you came round this evening. So we could talk about it."

One side of his mouth tipped into a slight smile. "How about we do a deal? One we both stick to this time."

"Okay."

"Instead of running away or getting into brawls, let's talk things through."

"I can live with that."

"In fact…" He kissed her again. "Talking is a good start but then…"

She ran her hands over his collarbones, around his neck and linked her fingers at his nape. "Then what?"

"Then it's hugely overrated." In one swift move, he hoisted her into the air and set his hands on her buttocks.

Megan gasped and wrapped her legs around his waist as her shoulders pressed into the wall again.

He grinned and pushed against her.

Megan giggled. "So what are you suggesting?"

"Can't you guess?"

"No, I think you should show me." She pulled him close for a hungry kiss, letting him know that she loved him too, even if she hadn't said it yet. But she would soon, because it was overflowing in her heart.

"'Oh, well…I… Hello…"

Megan broke the kiss at the sound of Georgie's voice.

James spun to face the door.

Megan didn't, instead she buried her head in his neck and laughed.

"I guess you must be James?" Georgie said, shutting the door with a click.

"I…um…yes…" he stammered. "I was just… I mean…"

Megan giggled harder. She wasn't used to hearing her big, tough, award-winning director at a loss for words.

After a few moments she decided to relieve him of his tortured embarrassment and unwrapped herself from him. He allowed her to slip to her feet but kept her near.

"Georgie," she said, turning to her best friend, who looked

like the cat who'd got the cream. "Meet James Carter, my…"

"Boyfriend, yes I know." She smiled and stepped forward with her hand held out. "Nice to meet you at last. I've heard all about you."

"Oh, all good I hope." James released Megan momentarily to shake hands with Georgie but then held her close again immediately afterwards.

"So, so," Georgie said with a wink and flicked her hand from side to side. "Hadn't heard that breaking and entering was on your skill list though."

"I didn't." He looked at Megan and a fleeting flash of alarm crossed his face. "I was just waiting outside to see Megan and — "

Georgie laughed and banged him on the arm. "I'm messing with you. If Megan is pleased that you're here, and by the looks of it she is, then so am I. Come on, let's get the kettle on." She dumped her purse on the side and walked past them into the kitchen.

James pressed his forehead to Megan's and groaned quietly.

"What?" Megan whispered, smiling.

"That could have been considerably more embarrassing."

"Why?" She had a pretty good idea.

He swept his lips over hers. "Well to be honest I had no plans on finding a bedroom. Right here, against the wall was going to work just fine."

14

"It's another beautiful day," Megan said, standing at the kitchen sink and looking out over their small courtyard.

The brilliant white sun overhead was already eating up the shadows and the flowers held their faces bravely to the heat.

"Get used to it," James said, winding his arms around her waist and pulling her back to his chest. "It's always like this in LA."

"I think I could."

He kissed the side of her neck. "Good."

"Blimey, would you two get a room," Georgie said with a laugh.

"Sorry." Megan made no move to untangle herself from James. She loved being close to him, the closer the better and the more often the better too. How could they have let such a stupid little thing like Tate Simmons come between them? "But the thing is, Brendon and I have had to put up with you and Tom all loved-up for months, this is just pay back."

"Ahh, Tom." James stepped away and picked up his tea.

Megan missed him instantly.

"He's your fiancé, is that right?" James asked.

"Yes. That's right. We're getting married soon."

"Congratulations."

"Thank you." She glanced at her phone. "I should call him."

"Your phone bill is going to be huge," Megan said.

"I know but I can't help myself."

"Thank goodness you're seeing him tomorrow."

"Oh, are you heading home?" James asked, looking at Georgie over the rim of his mug and leaning back on the

173

counter.

"Yes. I've got work to attend to, plus…"

"You couldn't be without Tom for another day," Megan finished for her.

Georgie shrugged and looked unapologetic. "Well, that's how love is, right. It's almost painful to be apart."

Megan walked over and reached for her hand. "Thank you so much for coming over to LA. It meant the world to me to have you there for the launch and my birthday. Such a wonderful surprise, I'll never forget it."

"Wouldn't have missed it for all the tea in China." Georgie smiled and squeezed her hand.

The click of the front door caught Megan's attention.

Brendon.

He'd been out all night.

"Well, love a duck, what have we here?" he said, strutting into the room. "Looking cosy, cosy, cosy." He winked at James.

"You're a dirty stop out," Georgie said before James needed to respond.

"Is there any other way to be a stop out?" Brendon said then cackled. "Would be a total waste to be a *clean* stop out."

Megan started to form an argument to that but silenced herself. What was the point? Brendon was incorrigible, but also, by the looks of it, very happy. "So Zane was good company?"

"The best, and…" Brendon dumped a bag of bagels on the table. They smelled divine. "He's coming over tonight. Party here, right…to say goodbye to our Georgie." He nodded at James. "You up for a party, sir?"

"Absolutely." James grinned at Brendon then at Megan. "Wouldn't miss it."

Megan felt a lovely glow spread through her, like honey on warm toast. She might be thousands of miles from her home, an ocean from her family but the people in this room, they made that all okay. Having James with her as well as Brendon and Georgie was perfect.

"Right, so, the plan is here for eight." Brendon looked at his watch. "We'll get takeout and pop some beers." He put on a strong, fake American accent. "What do y'all reckon?"

"Sounds great," Georgie said. "Are you still taking me to Rodeo Drive?"

"Yes of course, go get showered, chop, chop." Brendon jabbed his thumb over his shoulder then looked at Megan. "What are you planning for the day?"

Georgie ignored Brendon's instructions and reached into his bag for a bagel.

Megan looked at James. "I expect you're due on set soon, are you?"

"Nope." He shook his head. "Day off. Cooling down time. Besides…" He had the decency to look a little embarrassed. "Tate needs to let the swelling on his cheek reduce before we carry on shooting."

Megan reached up and touched the bruise on James' face. "I'm more worried about yours."

"Don't be. I'm tough." He leaned down and touched the tip of his nose to hers.

"Oh, for goodness sake," Brendon said, throwing his arms in the air. "Not you too, Megan, it's bad enough coping with all this slushy stuff from our Georgie."

Megan giggled. "'Fraid so." She didn't take her attention from James.

James grinned. "I've got a late afternoon appointment with my boss at the studio."

"About the fight?" Megan asked, suddenly worried that he'd got into terrible trouble over her.

"No, nothing like that. I'm pitching an idea for another documentary. Need to hand it in personally so that I know it gets to the board as soon as possible."

"Oh, okay. Will you be okay to join us at eight?"

"Yes, of course. And I'm free before that meeting." He swept his tongue over his bottom lip. "Have you been on the Ferris wheel yet? The one at the end of the pier?"

"No." Megan shook her head. "Why?"

"Neither have I, and I hear it's the done thing to do." He pulled her close.

"Well I'd love to, but..." Megan glanced at Georgie. She really should be maximizing her time with her best friend. But...

"Go..." Georgie shooed her with her hand. "I want to do Rodeo with Brendon this morning and we'll have all afternoon and evening together. Make the most of James having an unexpected day off."

"Are you sure?"

"Yes, absolutely."

Megan turned back to James. "Well in that case, it's a date."

🌴 🌴 🌴

An hour later, Megan and James were strolling past the cafés, popcorn vendors and spinning rides that led the way to the end of Santa Monica Pier. A roller coaster rattled in the distance and the tinny music from an arcade game pierced the air.

Megan linked her arm with James' and looked around at the people milling about. Everyone seemed to be excited, as if they were in holiday mode. Funny how stepping onto a pier with fairground attractions did that.

"Do you want an ice cream?" James asked, pointing to a white cart shaded by a bright umbrella. A woman in a tight red sarong style dress and a straw hat was scooping sweet treats into small white pots.

"Mmm, yes please," Megan said, licking her lips.

"What flavour?" James steered them safely past a skateboarder and up to the stand.

"Let's see what's on offer." Megan feasted on the sight of so many wonderful looking choices—mint, strawberry, vanilla, mocha—what should she have? "I can't decide."

James laughed. "It is hard. Mmm...let me see. I think I'll go with Tutti Fruitti."

"That looks nice." Megan wondered if she should have the same but the mango and passion fruit was really calling her.

"What can I get you?" the woman in the straw hat asked.

"I think I'll have mango and passion fruit," Megan said, making a sudden decision.

"And one of those." James pointed to his choice.

Megan felt her phone vibrate in her purse. She reached for it and checked the screen. "It's Enid," she said to James. "I should take it just in case there's a problem."

"Of course." James flipped open his wallet. "Go ahead."

"Hi, Enid, everything okay?" She glanced at the time – it was morning in London.

"Megan, I'm glad I've caught you, are you okay to talk?"

"Yes, of course." She paused. "What's up?"

"Well, nothing really."

Megan could tell by her voice that something was amiss. Her secretary was usually a fast, efficient talker who got straight to the point.

"It's silly…" Enid added.

"I'm sure it isn't, not if you're worried enough to call." Megan walked to the rail at the side of the pier and stared out at the long beach heading north, strung with desirable residencies, including James'. "Enid."

"Well it's just this strange thing happened, a few days ago."

"Oh." Megan was getting more and more confused. "What?"

"Well, I got in, early as usual to be on top of things before it hit nine, and in the way I always do I popped on the kettle. I can't function without at least two cups of tea in me." She paused and laughed but it was strained.

Megan waited for her to continue.

"But," Enid said, "there was no milk, I'd forgotten to pick some up from home. I'd noticed, though, that one of the estate agent boys next door was in early too, lovely lads, aren't they?"

177

"Yes, they are." Megan had no idea where this conversation was going.

"So I popped round, just for a second you know, to get a cup of milk from them. I didn't chat or linger, just milk, a promise to replace and back. But then…"

James came to stand next to Megan. He held two pots of ice cream. "Is everything okay?" he mouthed.

Megan shrugged and held up one palm. "Enid. I think you should just tell me."

"It was a man," she said quickly. "When I came back there was a man in your office."

"A man."

"Yes, I hadn't been gone for more than a minute. I'd left the door open, I'm so sorry."

"It's okay, it's okay." Megan could tell she was upset. "What did he want? Did he steal anything?"

"No, no nothing like that. He was quite friendly really, chatty. Wanted to know how Winter Shoes was going. He was leafing through paperwork and some samples I had packed up ready to send to you when I arrived. He didn't seem interested in the shoes, in the end products, just well…you."

A sinking feeling landed in Megan's chest. "Just interested in me." She looked at James who'd started on his ice cream. "Enid, what did he look like?"

"Tall, messy brown hair, vesty top and sweat pants."

"Did he give a name?"

"No, I asked him and he dodged the question and went off with a wave, like he was feeling pretty smug with himself."

Oh God. Dylan?

Megan felt her heart rate pick up. Thank goodness she was thousands of miles away from her office if her ex was still sniffing around like a crazed stalker.

But would it really have been him?

Who else could it have been? The description fit him perfectly.

Stay calm.

178

"But he didn't take anything?"

"No, he left emptied handed, cheerful enough with it. I suppose it just creeped me out a bit and I guessed it was best to tell you."

"Yes, thank you for that." Megan paused. "Well, hopefully, whoever it was has satisfied his curiosity and won't be bothered to come back, but in the meantime, just to be safe, lock the door, even when you're in, that way he won't be able to surprise you. And anything else you're worried about let me know, or better still, call the police."

"I just hope he didn't get a look at any of your newest designs — he could be a thief for another designer sent to snoop."

"I doubt it, probably just a loony fan, or someone I used to know."

"Yes, well, let's hope so and let's hope we don't have to involve the police." Enid sounded calmer. "I've just fired you off a load of emails that need attention today, just so you know to check. The advertising company Brendon hired to create next season's brochure have a sample for you to look at and there's one from *Cosmopolitan* who would like to do an interview as soon as possible with you."

"Okay, thanks. I'll go online and give them my attention as soon as possible. Have a nice day."

"You too, Megan."

Megan ended the call.

"Everything okay?" James asked, handing her a now slightly runny tub of ice cream.

"Yes, I think so. Enid just had a strange visitor to the office."

James frowned and cocked his head.

"Nothing to worry about, I'm sure." Megan smiled. "And Enid is more than capable of handling the situation back there." She didn't want Dylan, or thoughts of Dylan, to spoil this lovely moment on the pier with James. James was ten times more of a man than Dylan would ever be. "This looks gorgeous." She poked at her ice cream then ladled a big blob into her mouth. "Oh wow."

James smiled. "Good." He looked up the beach. "You can just see my place from here, right in the distance before that crag of rock."

"Oh yes." Megan peered up the shoreline. It was a truly spectacular place to live.

"You know you're welcome anytime," he said, leaning his behind on the railing and looking at her.

"Thanks. It's a beautiful house, I'll happily hang out there."

"Good, and as much as you want for as long as you want." He scraped the base of his pot and put the last dregs in his mouth.

"How long are you going to be here?" Megan asked. "Before you go off to document some other world event or injustice."

He took several paces to the right, dropped his rubbish in a bin then came back to stand next to her. "It all depends on whether my proposal gets accepted."

"The one you're handing in this afternoon?"

"Yes. I'm hoping to wrap up this thing with Tate within the week, editing will be minimal and then I'm free."

"That's good, that you're free."

"And that I won't have to see his face every day."

Megan laughed. "Most of the world enjoys seeing his face, but not you and I."

"No, not you and I." He bent and kissed her, his lips cool. "No more talk of him. Let's head to the Ferris wheel."

"Okay."

They ambled towards the end of the pier, Megan enjoying her ice cream and noticing the occasional admiring glance James received from other women. He seemed oblivious, which she thought was endearing. She wasn't surprised that he drew admiration—it was clear he had a sexy, toned body beneath his faded denims and black polo. And with a peppering of stubble from having spent the night at hers with no razor, he had a mysterious edge to his brooding look. In a city full of man-scaping, fakery and vanity, James' natural masculinity was both rare and appealing.

She finished her ice cream, disposed of the pot, then looked up at the majestic wheel.

"It's the only solar powered one in the world," James said. "I guess it makes sense to harness this energy."

"Wow, really. I didn't know that." Megan studied the swinging cages rotating past her. She looked up. "Goes pretty high."

"That's the idea. We'll get great views." He held out the two tickets he'd bought. The assistant took them.

They climbed into a red cage and sat on the same side. It rocked and swayed under their weight.

Megan giggled and gripped the rail. "Will it be okay?"

"Well, I'm heavy but you're light as a feather so I'm hoping we'll even it out."

"Stay seated at all times," the attendant said sternly, and shut the door with a clank.

James chuckled and put his arm around Megan's shoulders. He pulled her close.

She leaned against him and felt her tummy float as they began to drift upwards. The people on the pier grew smaller, the noise fainter. As the breeze picked up and ruffled her hair, she could see the endless blue expanse of ocean that hugged the LA coastline. "Wow!"

"Do you like it?"

"I love it, it's amazing." She twisted within his embrace to study the skyscrapers that were fogged with haze, then she looked down towards her temporary home and the guys that pumped iron in the heat of the day. "This was such a good idea."

"I'm glad you like it." He caught her face in his free hand and turned her to him. "The only view I really need is right here, though, right next to me."

She smiled and as she did so he kissed her. If her tummy wasn't already giddy with the ride, the sweetness of his kiss would have definitely sent it somersaulting.

"James," she said, breaking the kiss and holding his face the same way he was holding hers. "You know when you said that you loved me."

His expression fell serious. "It was the truth."

"Well..." She paused. The words were on her tongue, stacking up, waiting to be said. She had to say them. "I love you too."

Something seemed to melt in his eyes and he swept his tongue over his lips. "Baby..."

She silenced him with another kiss as the wheel spun them past the attendant on the ground then up again to what felt like the top of the world. Megan clung to him. Had she ever felt so happy? So in love? One thing was for sure, James was the best thing that had happened to her in a very long time and she wasn't letting go of him again, not for anything or anyone.

"Are you ready for this?" Brendon asked taking Megan's hands.

"Er, yes. I think so." She'd said goodbye to James an hour ago then headed back to the rented house in Venice Beach.

"You should probably sit down," Georgie said, shifting a pile of designer bags from the sofa to make room.

"Really? Can't you just tell me?"

"Well we could, sweetpea, but then we'd have to catch you when you toppled over."

Megan laughed and sat. She crossed her legs and looked between her two friends. Both had flushed cheeks and looked like they'd shopped hard.

"Well," Brendon started.

"While we were in LA Hype he had a phone call," Georgie finished.

"Oh, who from?" Megan asked.

"The show on Friday is confirmed, you're on the *Paul Piper* show."

Megan was aware of a shot of adrenaline hitting her veins. "Bloody hell."

"Yes, we must find you something fabulous to wear and I'm thinking those Silverdust shoes, what do you reckon?"

"Well yes—"

"But that's not all." Georgie was almost bouncing on the spot.

"It's not?" Megan asked

"No, there's a spare segment come up on Lafayette fashion show next week," Brendon said. "They do a special footwear section at the end and thanks to a nasty strain of pneumonia, Tristan Penton-Smythe can't make it."

"Oh dear." Megan downturned her mouth. That sounded nasty.

"He'll be fine." Brendon flicked his hand in the air. "Nothing antibiotics can't cure."

"It's not televised," Georgie went on, "but everyone who is anyone in the LA fashion world will be there, it will be great for you to make some contacts."

"And because it's after the *Paul Piper* show, you're free to dismiss any relationship with Tate Simmons, but they'll all know exactly who you are without you having to be introduced. They'll all want to talk to you, find out about you, and with that adorable British accent of yours, they'll be in love before the day is over."

"Wow, that is pretty amazing." Megan was glad she was sitting down. A TV interview then a fashion show would thrust her into the spotlight.

"It's more than amazing." Brendon grabbed Georgie's hands and began to spin her around.

Georgie went happily, kicking up her heels and whooping.

"You're going to be stratospheric, up there with the stars!" he shouted. "And all the stars will be wearing Winter Shoes."

"Winter Shoes," Georgie echoed then broke into peals of laughter as Brendon let her go and she bounced, dizzy, onto the sofa next to Megan.

Megan reached for her and hugged her close. She didn't want Georgie to go back to London but she couldn't ask her to stay. Besides, she knew how lucky she was to have two amazing friends.

15

James

Watching Megan walk away from him, down towards Venice Beach, hadn't been something he'd liked doing. He still hadn't moved from the pier. An ache in his chest told him to be with her, to have her at his side. He couldn't remember when he'd last felt like that about a woman, but wow, it had hit him hard with Megan.

There was just something about her…

Her sweet smile, her sexy body, the way he couldn't always predict what she was going to say or do. She was fun to be around, great company and he was excited for her about everything that seemed to be heading her way. It would be a privilege to stand by her and watch it all unfold and celebrate her successes with her.

He smiled to himself and swept his tongue over his bottom lip, trying to catch any flavour of her that lingered from their goodbye kiss earlier.

Mmm…maybe a hint of sweetness, like honey and sugar mixed with woman. She even tastes delicious.

But delicious as she was, Megan Winter had certainly had him running in circles a few times. He'd never have thought he'd be the type to lurk in bushes and brawl on the beach. But he had. What had come over him? Jealousy, that's what. He'd just seen red, blood-boiling red that had made him behave in a way he never normally would have. Tate Simmons had pushed him way too far, he'd discovered James' boundaries and what happened when they were crossed.

Hell, Tate had more than pushed, he'd ran straight over his boundaries, bashed them out of the way and grinned as he'd done it.

Prat.

If he'd known Megan would have been so upset by the incident, though, he maybe would have tried to rein in some of the fury that had circled in his veins. But he'd had no idea she'd be so affronted by him defending her honour. He'd thought it was the chivalrous thing to do — sort of.

He glanced at his watch. He'd see her again in a few hours. Eight o'clock wasn't that far away and he did need to give her some time alone with Georgie on her last day in LA, that was only fair. Tempting as it was to be selfish and keep her to himself, he knew that wasn't the way to behave.

He shoved his hands in his pockets and turned around. A woman on rollerblades, with earphones in and wearing a silvery bikini smiled at him.

He returned the smile but didn't hold her gaze. He wasn't interested in anyone else, only the girl he loved and who loved him right back. It didn't matter that LA was full of beautiful people, women he could easily date, take back to his bed for the night, he didn't want them. Never had. One-night stands weren't his thing, he liked love to be part of the equation.

A warm feeling swelled in his chest. Love. He loved Megan, and she loved him too. She'd said it right there on the Ferris wheel.

He glanced over at it jutting into the blue sky. He'd never forget that moment for as long as he lived. She'd said it from the heart, he knew she had. With her gaze set firmly on his, she'd looked into his soul and allowed him to look into hers.

He huffed and began walking. Since when had he had such soppy, romantic thoughts? That wasn't who he was — he was an award-winning investigative journalist, not some sappy teenager with a crush and a penchant for poetry.

Well, that was until Megan had come along. Now it seemed he was a man in love and anything went, as long as it involved her.

"Hey, James, great to see you."

"Hi, Rue, how's it going?" James stepped into his boss' office, clutching the carefully laid-out proposal document under his arm. It was cool, the air con working hard, and the blinds had been half drawn to keep out the harsh daylight.

Rue stood and came around his desk. He held out his hand.

James shook it.

"Ha, quite a shiner he gave you." Rue peered through his glasses and studied James' cheek. He frowned and tutted.

James twisted away and took a seat. "Well, I got him better."

"Don't I know it." Rue sounded mad but James knew he was amused by the whole incident. It was the first time James had ever messed up—he could afford one strike. "That's why there's no filming today and it's costing the studio money."

"He'll be okay to film tomorrow, as long as he behaves."

"Behaves, and by that you mean stay away from the woman who was on his arm at the award ceremony last week?" Rue retreated to the other side of his wide mahogany desk and sat in a large brown leather chair. "Megan Winter, isn't it?"

"Yep, and I think he's got the message to stay away from her." James could feel the hairs on the back of his neck prickling. He took a deep breath to calm himself down. It wouldn't be good to lose it with Rue, not when he needed him to okay this next project. It was essential that he had him on side.

He decided to change the subject. "Any news on Leo? Has he come off his bender yet? I wouldn't mind handing this damn *Baywatch* project back to him, he can edit it. Bloody thing is ridiculous."

Rue sat back and folded his arms. "Yep, he showed up in Vegas, got hauled in by the cops for being drunk and disorderly and groping a blackjack attendant."

"Classy."

"Are we surprised?" Rue shook his head. "And now he's in rehab, again. So I'm afraid you're stuck with this project to the bitter end."

James shrugged. "Well, I was kind of expecting that." He paused and placed his folder of papers on the table. He set his hand, fingers spread, over the top of it.

"And that is...?" Rue studied James over the rim of his glasses.

"My proposal, for the board. You said you'd present it favourably if I ponced around with this *Baywatch* documentary."

"Did I?"

"Yeah, and you know full well you did, Rue." James paused. "On the phone, when you dragged me back for this crap."

"Mmm, okay..."

"Remember?"

"Yes, yes, I remember, course I remember." Rue spoke slowly and reached for the information James was still holding flat to the table. "You going to let me read it or what?"

"Yeah, sure." James lifted his hand. "Naturally Grant is part of it. My cameraman. Wouldn't do it without him."

"Goes without saying, you're a mighty fine team." Rue lifted the folder and examined the first page. "Central America."

"Yep, not too far." James squirmed on his seat. The Middle East had been dangerous but at least they'd had an army behind them, literally. This part of the world they'd be on their own. And yes, it would be dangerous.

"Sounds a bit damn dangerous," Rue said, frowning. "Don't know if I want you both there."

"Not if we're sensible."

"Columbia, El Salvador, Nicaragua. Investigating drug lords and farmers forced to grow illegal substances or risk murder of them and their families."

"It's going on, right now. These people are slave labour yet the men that orchestrate the manufacture of cocaine are living the high life, like kings. I know I can't fight for better wages for creating an evil substance that ruins so many lives, but I can expose what's going on and hope the world's governments sit up and take notice."

Rue was quiet. He continued to read, still studying the proposal.

"What do you think?" James asked eventually, unable to stand the silence.

Rue looked up and slipped his glasses off. "Truth?"

"Yep, give it to me."

"I don't want you or Grant hanging out with these guys. What we'll be able to do to protect you will be very limited."

"I get that." James nodded and sat forward. "But—"

"But..." Rue held up his hand. "I do know that this sort of thing is right up your street and if anyone can do it then it's you and Grant."

"Yes, thank you." James felt a sprig of hope growing within him. "And with a few contacts I've already made, I think I can organise us protection."

"Military?" Rue looked confused.

"No, mercenaries."

Rue huffed. "I should have guessed. Only you would have connections for those sorts of guys."

"What can I say, they've come in handy in the past."

Rue held up his hand. "I don't want to know, especially if that was with studio money."

"All above board, you know me," James said then sat back again with a smirk.

"Mmm..." Rue fingered the proposal again.

"So you'll put it forward?"

"Yes, I said I would if you did this project for Walder and I'm a man of my word."

"And you'll sign it off first so the others follow suit."

Rue shut his eyes and squeezed the bridge of his nose.

"You really want to go to hell?"

"Hell on earth." James paused. Rue was right, from what he'd already looked into that was exactly where he'd be going. Swamps, mosquitos, armed militia, lawless farmers and that was before the alligators and murdering drug lords set to work. There would be no five-star hotel, no restaurant for a slap-up meal at the end of the day—it would be all about survival on every level and telling the story. "Yes, I'm sure. *We're* sure." He set his jaw tight, this was it, what they wanted to do.

Rue sighed. "You're the only damn producer who scares the shit out of me, you know that. I can cope with the ones that fall of the wagon, end up in bed with other people's wives and even enjoy a bit of coke taking themselves, but you...you always push it, James Carter."

"And it wins me awards." James tried not to sound too smug about that but he was still pleased.

"Yeah, congratulations again on that. I'm sorry I couldn't make it that night. Wife's birthday, big celebration planned, you know how it is."

"How is Diane?"

"She's great, planning her next charity event, on a yacht, would you believe. Gets more and more elaborate to get cash out of people." He paused. "Hey, you should come."

"Well, I don't know..."

"As our celebrity guest. There's people there who'd love to chat to you about your win and your work."

James laughed. "Well, now I really don't know, I'm hardly a celebrity."

"No, but that pretty lady of yours is."

James bit on his bottom lip.

Rue chuckled. "You cleverly deflected the conversation away from Megan Winter but I'm not a dumb-ass. Only a man in love would take out another guy in front of a whole crowd just for swatting her ass."

James swallowed. His love life was nothing to do with his work at the studio.

"Oh, I know you're very private, son, but you threw that in the air for this one. Everyone's seen Tate Simmons being taken down a peg or two for disrespecting Ms Winter and it doesn't take a genius to know she's more than a passing fling for you." He tipped his head. "I'm right, aren't I?"

James sighed. "Yes, she's very much part of my life. From what I gather, Tate used her to get back at an ex, some rock chick I've never heard of. But now they have nothing between them."

"Well" — Rue stood — "I'm glad to hear it because you deserve someone special in your life and she sure looks sweet."

James couldn't help the smile that spread on his face. "She is, very."

Rue laughed and walked around the desk. He rested his hand on James' shoulder. "So bring her to the yacht event, she'll love it, and I for one would like to meet the woman that has finally stolen your heart, and I know Diane would too."

She'd certainly done that.

"Okay, I'll ask her. Thanks." James also stood. "And the proposal?"

"Well, I'll put it to the board with my full backing behind it. I can tell it means a lot to you and I know what you're like once you have an idea, you're like a terrier after a rat, you just won't give it up."

James shrugged. "I want what I want."

"And don't I know it. The only thing is, what's your lovely new lady going to say about armed drug gangs chasing you through swamps?"

"Oh she'll be fine about it."

I hope.

James made his way out of the studios and took a cab towards Venice Beach. It was only seven and he had some time to kill, plus he needed to call Grant and give him the low-down on the meeting with Rue.

He spotted a bar, First Base, and ducked into its shady

interior. He found a free stool at the end and sat. A wide screen TV was showing a baseball match with the sound muted.

"What can I get you?" asked the barman.

"Coors, thanks," James replied then pulled out his mobile. He called up Grant's number. "Hey, mate."

"How did it go?"

"Great, Rue went for it. Not best pleased about the safety aspects but what could he do, he'd promised me this if I covered for Walder."

"That was a useful tool."

"So it's going to the board next month, though hopefully he'll get it passed sooner."

"Yeah, he won't want us hanging around doing nothing until then. Waste of studio money."

James ran his hand through his hair and glanced at the guy next to him. He wore a Yankee cap and shades even though it was dim in the bar. He was picking at the label on his beer and staring at the baseball game on screen.

"He's invited me to some charity event on a yacht too. Wants me to schmooze." James clicked his tongue on the roof of his mouth.

Grant chuckled. "Oh go, and take Megan, she'll love it."

"Yeah, I probably will. Right, best go now, I'm off to see her soon, well, in about an hour."

"Ah, listen to you, counting the hours till you're together again. You just can't bear to be without her, your heart can't beat unless you're together…"

"Grant."

"What?"

"You're a dick, you know that." James smiled and ended the call.

"There you go." The bartender set a beer in front of James.

"Cheers." James took a long drink. It had been a good day.

"Another English accent. I like it."

James turned to the man next to him, who was obviously

English himself.

"Yes, long way from home, right." James smiled.

"It is, and the jetlag is a bummer. Can't decide if it's day or night."

"Well, it's most certainly evening," James said. "You on holiday?"

"Sort of. Business too, personal business, you get my drift?"

"Lots of different types of business." James glanced at the screen as a cheer went round the bar. Clearly the popular team were winning.

"You get this baseball shit?"

"No, not my thing." James shrugged.

"What is your thing?" The man studied James.

James couldn't see his eyes through his glasses.

"I'm sorry. You want a quiet drink and I'm jabbering on."

"No, it's fine," James said. "We Brits should stick together." He smiled. "My thing is work, it's consuming though…" He paused. "There is a special lady in my life now, that's making it worth coming home for."

"Aren't you the lucky one?"

"Yes, I think so."

"You love her."

"I do indeed."

There was a pause, then, "Why?"

"Why?" James frowned — it was an odd question. "Because she's beautiful inside and out, she's talented, fun to be with, she drives me crazy and she makes me feel complete. Like I'd do anything in the world for her."

Wow! Where has all that come from?

It was official, he was going soft. Just as well only a stranger had heard that embarrassing gush.

"Ah, you enjoy it, mate. I had love like that once, but lost it."

"Sorry to hear that."

The man shrugged, his faded denim jacket bunching around his ears. "I'm not one to admit defeat though. I want her back and I'm going to do that. It's just taking a little longer than I thought."

"Are you still with her?"

"Nah, she left me, but that's okay." The stranger tapped the side of his nose. "I have a cunning plan."

James drained the last of his beer. Talking of Megan had just made him feel all the more desperate to be with her. "Well good luck with that," he said, sliding from the stool.

His phone rang. He glanced at the screen.

Megan.

"Hi, sexy," he said.

"Hi, sexy, yourself."

He smiled and fished a few dollar bills from his wallet.

"Why don't you come round early, if you can? We're just sifting through takeout menus."

"Actually that will suit me fine. I'm not far away."

"Great, see you soon."

"Yep."

"And, James…"

"Yes?"

"Don't be long. I've missed you this afternoon."

"I've missed you too, baby." He ended the call.

"That her?" asked the guy.

"Yes, I'm heading there now."

"I can see she makes you happy."

"Happier than I thought possible." James held out his hand.

The man took it and shook.

"I hope it works out for you, mate," James said. "With the girl."

"Oh it will. I have a good feeling about it."

16

Megan

Megan set her phone on the table next to the sofa and hugged her arms around herself. James would be here soon. He'd said that he was nearby.

As far as she was concerned, he couldn't get there fast enough. She'd missed him desperately all afternoon. How could she have ever contemplated that they were over? That was just ridiculous.

But if it hadn't been for his insistence that they talk about it, if he hadn't lurked in the bushes and quite literally ambushed her, she might be sitting alone and broken-hearted right now.

Except she wasn't alone. She was with Georgie and Brendon in their lovely rental home and now Zane had just turned up too.

Zane was great and a perfect match for Brendon. They even wore similar clothes and had matching stiff-quiffed hairstyles. It was clear they were into each other and it wasn't just a passing fling—or at least Megan hoped it wasn't—because it was high time that Brendon found someone to spend his life with. Someone who was kind and considerate of his feelings and not just up for the fun. Because Brendon was fun to be around, he was like a ray of sunshine, a ball of hyperactivity, and for that reason he could be high-maintenance. In the past, Megan had worried his bouncing attention span and love of partying had put boyfriends off. But luckily Zane seemed of a similar energy level and had equally fast-paced chains of thought. She hoped he'd be able to keep up with Brendon's flittering mind, his passions that bordered on obsessive and his crazy ideas that always seemed to pan out well somehow.

She looked around the room. Georgie was busy wrapping several shirts she'd bought for Tom from Rodeo Drive. She wanted to surprise him as soon as he picked her up from Heathrow. She'd gone a little over the top with gifts for him, and Megan was sure she'd buy him cologne, booze and chocolate from the airport too. They were guilt buys and it made Megan feel a bit bad that Georgie had been made to pick between her and her fiancé for her holiday. But they'd be back together soon, planning the big day and getting excited about all the little details. Then of course they'd have a honeymoon too, somewhere lovely and sunny where they could lounge about together and sip piña coladas.

"He's going to love that pale blue one," Megan said. "It will really suit his colouring."

"Yes, I think so." Georgie tipped her head and smoothed down the collar almost as if Tom were already wearing it. "Maybe he'll pick it for it this weekend. We're going to visit my cousin in Chelsea — she's just bought a new place."

"Oh, the one that needed a lot of work doing to it?"

"Yes, with the attic extension."

"Sounded like a money pit, didn't they have damp in the cellar too?"

"Yes, but it's all fixed and the whole place is finished now. She wants to show it off. She's planned a barbecue with a paddling pool for the kids and all the family are going."

"Let's hope it's nice weather then," Megan said. "So that you're not all stuck in the house."

"Yes, let's hope so. I've been spoilt here," Georgie said, "sun, sun and more sun. I could get used to it. The warmth agrees with my asthma and my mood." She rubbed her hand down her tanned arm. "And it's nice to not be so damn pale."

"So move out here with us." Megan grinned. "That would be cool."

Georgie was quiet for a moment, a slight frown marring

her forehead. "How long are you planning on staying here in LA, Megan? Do you know yet?"

Megan knew that was always going to be something she'd have to face. From the second she'd booked a one-way ticket and run away from London, James and Dylan. Well, James was here now but that was okay, more than okay and she had no intention of running anywhere away from him again. But still, she'd always known that a return trip would have to be booked at some point. She wasn't a US citizen, she couldn't stay indefinitely, going home would have to be faced. "I can stay three months on a temporary visa, after that they'll send me packing." She shrugged.

"And will that be long enough to raise the Winter Shoes' flag over LA?"

"I hope so."

"Of course it will," Brendon butted in. "We're already halfway there."

"Plus there's the fabulous Greta Breen who's already agreed to wear Megan's designs for the Oscars in February." Zane held up his hand. "Not a small thing by any stretch of the imagination."

"That's so awesome, Zane," Georgie said. "Like really bloody awesome to have organised that."

"*You're* awesome," Brendon took Zane's hand and gave it a squeeze.

"Well I'm not going to argue with that." Zane laughed and bumped his shoulder against Brendon's.

"Talking of awesome and awards, where is your hunky man, Megan?"

"I just spoke to him, he'll be here soon." Megan tucked her hair behind her ears then reached into her bag. She applied a sweep of red lipstick and a squirt of perfume. She'd already showered and pulled on a pale pink sundress but still, she wanted to look her best for the man she loved.

"Where did he have to dash to again?" Georgie asked. "Sorry, I should remember but I was just so excited about going to Rodeo Drive again to buy stuff for Tom."

"That's okay." Megan smiled. "He went to the studio. He's putting in a proposal for his next documentary. It needs to get funding and approval and all kinds of other important stuff from the board." He had told her the details of the application process but she couldn't really remember, she'd been too busy studying his mouth as he'd spoken, wondering when she'd next be able to steal a kiss. She really should try harder to listen...

"What's it about, this next documentary?" Zane asked. "Or are we not allowed to know yet?"

"I don't think it's a secret." Megan paused. "He mentioned something about drugs." She hesitated, remembering the conversation they'd had at the Italian restaurant back in London. Again the details in her mind were vague but she could recall feeling uncomfortable and that she'd thought it sounded terribly risky. She'd hoped at the time that a different project would come along for him, which it had in the form of the lifeguard documentary, but now...now that was coming to an end he was bound to go seeking out his next adventure.

"Megan?" Brendon asked.

"Sorry, I was just thinking about what he'd said."

Adventure!

"Which was?" Georgie asked.

"Yes, drugs, and war lords and exposing them, that's what he said. Though I hope he's switched it to something else, or at least that he's not planning on heading to Central America anymore." A shiver went up her spine and a weight grew in her belly. "That sounds too dangerous. There must be other stuff he can go and film with Grant. Different projects he could get involved in that would suit him." She sighed. "Though it does sound like he gets himself into these things."

"What do you mean?" Georgie asked.

"Well he's been to Afghanistan and into war zones in the past. It seems danger is a bit of a theme for him."

Georgie rested her hand on Megan's knee. "I'm sure it

will all be fine."

Megan couldn't shake the bad feeling or relax the frown from her brow.

"Yes, only worry about the stuff you can change, sweetpea, and the rest" — Brendon did a swooshing motion over his head — "let that all float away, it's not good for your karma. Like this...gone, gone, gone."

"Mmm...yes," Megan said, trying to imagine her worries floating away. "You're right."

"I'm always right," Brendon said, giving her a wink. "And you know it."

"The pressing matter is, though," Zane said, holding out the flats of his palms. "What are you wearing to the *Paul Piper* show on Friday, Megan? You know of course that LA Hype is at your absolute disposal. Come in and try the whole shop on. Anything you fancy at all, just say the word."

"Thank you, that's very kind." Megan smiled. "Really, so kind."

"Oh, oh, oh..." Brendon bounced on the sofa. "That dove grey dress with the diamante straps, it would go perfectly with the Silverdust shoes." He looked between Zane, Georgie and Megan with excitement on his face. "Don't you all agree? Perfect."

Megan thought of the shoes Brendon had just mentioned. They were silver with crystals set in the heels and on the straps which crossed halfway up her calves. She needed something plain and complementary. The shoes had to be the star of the show, or at least the star of her outfit — she didn't want an overbearing dress. "Let me see it," she said. "But I trust Brendon's judgement if he's already thinking it's perfect, then I'll more than likely go with it."

"Yes, he has exceptional taste," Zane said.

Brendon poked him in the ribs. "That's why I'm with you."

Zane wriggled then laughed. "Indeed."

"*Now* who needs to get a room," Megan said feigning

annoyance and rolling her eyes.

"Did Enid get in touch with you?" Georgie asked suddenly.

"Er, yes, why?"

"No reason, she called me earlier, that's all." Georgie applied the last bit of tape to the gift she was wrapping and set it aside. "She'd tried to call you but no luck. You must have been otherwise engaged with James." She winked.

"Oh, I didn't notice a missed call."

"It doesn't matter." Georgie shrugged. "As long as she got hold of you in the end."

"Yes…it was weird, though." Megan sat back on the sofa and crossed her legs.

"What was?" Georgie frowned.

"She said that a few days ago, she'd popped next door to the estate agents to get some milk for her tea and—"

"Phew, I love those guys," Brendon said, fanning his face. "They smell so nice. Not a queer one amongst them but still, they're easy on the eye and the nose."

Zane giggled.

"One track minds." Georgie rolled her eyes. "Go on, Megan."

"She said that when she came back there was a bloke in the office. Tall a bit scruffy, wearing sweats and vesty top."

"Who was it?" Georgie looked baffled.

"She said he wouldn't give his name, but he'd been poking around, looking at paperwork on the desk and that."

"Weird," Brendon said.

"Yup," Zane agreed. "Weird."

"What else?" Georgie asked.

"She said he didn't take anything or seem like he was going to. That he was just interested in me, wanted to know where I was, what I was doing and when I'd be back and stuff."

"Which she wouldn't have told him." Georgie nodded seriously. She'd handpicked Enid to be Megan's PA and would expect nothing but discretion from her. "She's very professional."

"No, of course not. She didn't give him any information at all." Megan frowned. "But she said he went then, just slipped out as if he had what he wanted, which was apparently nothing."

"So who was it?" Zane asked.

Megan looked between Brendon and Georgie. She knew the answer to that but still didn't really want to admit it. Once she did it would be out there. She pulled in a deep breath. "Dylan," she said.

"Dylan!" Georgie yelled. "No."

"Shit," Brendon gasped, his hand flying to his mouth. "Really? He's still lurking about? Are you sure?"

"Who else would it be?" Megan shrugged, resigned. "He'd obviously gone looking for me, found I wasn't there and had a poke about to see if he could find any clues to my whereabouts."

"Thank goodness you're here, thousands of miles away from him," Georgie said, putting her arm around Megan's shoulder and pulling her close. "I couldn't stand to leave and think that he was nearby. He was so damn freaky and possessive, wasn't he? Wouldn't take no for an answer."

"I just wish he'd give up," Megan said, shaking her head and knotting her fingers in her lap. "Why can't he just move on with his life? Find someone new like I have. He's going to have to accept it one day."

"He didn't take getting jilted well, that's for sure." Brendon sighed.

"Who would?" Zane said.

"True," Brendon agreed.

"But he didn't take anything from the office and Enid didn't tell him anything about you?" Georgie repeated.

"No, nothing."

"So he's still in the dark that you're here?" Brendon added.

"Presumably, though I'm not exactly incognito, not after the whole Tate Simmons thing. I might not have got to tell the world who I was but my face was on enough screens and photographs."

"Bloody hell. I bet that made his blood boil if he saw pictures of you two together looking all gorgeous and sexy," Brendon said. "Talk about going up in the world. Well, you know what I mean, in terms of fame and fortune. Dylan to Tate Simmons, not exactly a shoddy rebound, is it?"

"Not that I'm with Tate," Megan added quickly. "And never really was."

"Well we know that." Brendon held out his hands. "Chill."

"And I doubt he reads the gossip magazines and he rarely goes online." Megan shrugged. It didn't really matter. She couldn't care less if Dylan saw her with other men, in fact it might make him realise that she was getting on with her life and that he had no claim on her anymore.

"But I bet his sister does, or any one of his friends' girlfriends. They all know you, they'll have shown him that you're with Tate Simmons."

Megan shook her head. "I'll be glad to get on this damn show and put the world straight. *I am not with Tate Simmons.*"

"Shh, we know, we know." Georgie rubbed a soothing circle on her back. "And Friday will come round soon enough."

"Yeah, so don't sweat it any more tonight," Brendon said. "This is meant to be Georgie's leaving party, where the heavens is the party spirit? Did it just get up and waft away like an uninvited ghost?"

Megan looked at Georgie. "I'm sorry. Come on." She stood. "Let's get this show on the road. We need music." She set her iPhone in the docking station and put on a fast tune. She swayed her hips and clapped then spun in a circle.

"And food, I'm starving," Zane said over the music.

"Good plan, what does everyone want?" Brendon picked up a pile of takeout menus.

"Can we wait for James? He'll be here soon." Megan reached for Georgie's hands and pulled her standing.

"We'll dance till he gets here." She grinned. "Work up an appetite."

"I'm all for that." Georgie laughed, raised her hands in the air and began to sway her hips to the beat.

Megan danced around her then bumped her hip into Georgie's behind.

Georgie laughed harder and bumped her back.

Brendon jumped up, Zane too.

A wild dance around the living room ensued. Heels kicked up, whoops of delight echoed and the music got louder.

Megan felt high on life. This was it. So much was happening and it was all here and now. She didn't care about Dylan. He was a small, distant part of her life. Soon she'd be known in the fashion industry for the shoes she was so proud of and not for being on Tate's arm. Soon James would be here, and she would be very proud to be on his arm. Yes, life was good, it was all working out, and what's more, she was in love.

Over the din of the music she heard the doorbell. "Wait, hang on," she said breathlessly.

The others carried on dancing, taking no notice of her dashing from the room.

She pushed her hair from her forehead and straightened her top. Rushing to the door, she set a smile on her face. She pulled it open.

"Hi," she said.

"Hi, yourself." James took in her appearance. "Are you working out?"

"Dancing, come and join in." She reached for his hand and dragged him into the house. "It's a party!"

He laughed and kicked the door shut.

"Yay, it's Hot Guy," Brendon shouted as James entered the room.

Megan reached for a throw cushion and chucked it at him.

Brendon laughed and caught it. He grabbed Zane and swung him around with increased vigour.

"Hey, James, show us your moves," Georgie said, shimmying her hips as though she was a prize belly dancer.

"I'm afraid I don't have moves like that," James said then laughed.

"Ah, I bet you do." Megan pressed herself against him and wriggled to the beat.

He set a kiss to her lips and moved with her, wrapping her in his arms as he did so.

On and on they all danced. Georgie switched the music and grabbed Zane for a raunchy tango that consisted of him mainly pushing her away and snapping her close with a stern expression on his face.

Brendon took photos, cackling with delight as he examined each one. "These are all going on Facebook."

The doorbell ringing again broke the hysteria and sliced through the energy in the room.

"Whoa, that's me beat," Georgie said, flopping onto the sofa and wiping her forearm over her forehead. Her cheeks were flushed and she was breathing hard. Her top had become squint.

"Me too." Zane dropped down next to her and wiped at his own brow.

The bell rang again, tinkling through the hallway.

"Who *is* that?" Brendon said.

"Did you order takeout yet?" James asked. "Maybe it's food."

"No, we were waiting for you," Georgie replied. "On Megan's insistence."

"Ah, you're so thoughtful." He stroked her hair. "Thank you."

"I try." Megan untangled herself from him. "I'll get it, it might be next door. He said he was going away soon and asked if we would we water his plants."

James released her, and Megan wandered into the hallway. She blew out a breath. She was even more hot and bothered now than she'd been when James had arrived. She loved to dance and it didn't matter whether it was at home

204

or in a club. It was all fun, and good for her soul. Dancing made her feel better.

She undid the latch and swung it open, expecting to see their elderly next-door neighbour.

But it wasn't him.

Before her stood a person she did recognise, though. A man she'd thought was thousands of miles away. A man who'd doted on her, controlled her and now scared her.

"Dylan!" She clasped her hand over her mouth. Her legs didn't feel like her own and her stomach rolled. He wore a tattered T-shirt with a pair of shades poked into the collar and a Nike cap.

"Hi, honeypie, missed me?"

Sparkling Stilettos

Excerpt

Chapter One

Megan

"Oh my goodness, darling, you look fabulous. Utterly… totally…bloody fabulous."

Megan held her full champagne flute to Brendon's and they chinked rims, the sound tinkling around the plush West London hotel room.

"Thank you," she said then hesitated with the glass by her lips. She stared in the mirror at her unfamiliar bridal reflection. With her dark hair piled high, her makeup natural and long, dangling silver earrings, she hardly recognised herself. "But do you think it's maybe a bit over the top, you know, with the tiara?"

"No, no, not at all," Brendon said, shoving his hand on his waist and jutting out his left hip. "You, my beauty, are a princess, so of course you should be wearing a bejewelled crown." He tutted and tapped the base of her stem. "Sup, sup, it's your wedding day, champers needs to be drunk from dawn till dusk."

"Yes, but not too much," Georgie said with a smile but also a hint of sternness in her tone. "We don't want you sloshed as you walk down the aisle, Megan. You've got towering heels to keep control of. Beautiful, bespoke heels yes, I agree, but still, they're high even for you."

Megan took a deep breath and curled her toes into the soft beige carpet—her feet were a little cold even though the room was warm. In one hour she would be wearing the stunning new heels she'd designed and walking down the aisle to marry Dylan Dunkin-Buckshaw—yes, she would be Mrs Megan Rose Dunkin-Buckshaw and damn proud to be.

She could live with the name. Of course she could. She'd be sad to say goodbye to Winter, though, because Megan Rose Winter had a nice ring to it. But she'd used the name Winter to set up her beloved shoe design business a few years before, so if she looked at it like that, she wasn't really giving up her name. She'd still have it, and still use it on a daily basis. The only difference would be that her driving licence and bank account would say Dunkin-Buckshaw. But what did that matter? Who ever saw a person's licence or bank account? Well, Dylan would see her bank account now. He'd said they'd pool their cash once married— apparently that was what couples did after tying the knot.

"Are you sure you're not going for the red?" Brendon held up her scarlet MAC lipstick. It was her favourite, the only one she wore. But today she'd decided not to. Today she was going for nude gloss.

"No." She shook her head. "Dylan doesn't really like it. He says it's..." She paused, remembering the conversation.

"What?" Georgie fussed with a tendril of Megan's hair that had escaped. "What does he say?"

"Yes, tell us?" Brendon added with a frown. "I'm curious

now."

"He thinks it's a bit tarty."

Georgie gasped and shook her head. "No!"

Brendon slapped his hand over his mouth and widened his eyes.

"He said that?" Georgie asked. "He actually, really and truly said that?"

Megan shrugged. It was no big deal. He was entitled to have an opinion.

"But you've worn that shade for years." Brendon tutted. "It's so...you. It's your signature lippy."

"And it suits you so well, highlights the pretty shape of your mouth," Georgie added.

"Thank you, but it's just for today."

"Are you sure?" Brendon asked. "Because if you never wear it again I'll be heartbroken. In fact, I may as well just lie down here right now and die." He gestured to the four-poster bed then made a show of falling back onto it. He threw his arms over his face. "Oh, goodbye to the scarlet lips that we know and love. How can I go on?"

"Don't be so dramatic, it's only lipstick." Megan laughed. "Come on. Help me with the dress."

Georgie glanced at her iPhone. "Yes, you should get dressed. Time is ticking away. The bells will soon be ringing."

Megan stood. Her stomach was heavy even though she hadn't been able to eat that morning. Nerves, most likely. This was, after all, the biggest day of her life—or so she'd been told. If she wasn't nervous there'd be something wrong with her, right? If there were no butterflies swarming she'd be abnormal. Every bride had this sensation, she'd read about it, seen it in movies.

"How does this feel?" Georgie asked, adjusting the ties on the back of the white basque Megan wore. "Too tight?"

"No it's fine. It kind of feels like it's holding me together." Megan huffed at her silliness but it was the truth. With all the emotions rolling about inside her—apprehension, excitement, awestruck — the basque was like wearing a hug. It was comforting and made her feel secure.

"Your new husband will love that later," Brendon said, crawling off the bed and nodding approvingly. His gaze took in Megan standing in her sexy underwear. "My, my, if I wasn't into men, my sweetpea, I'd do you."

"Well thanks, I think." Megan giggled and reached for a pack of unopened white stockings.

"Who are you kidding, Brendon?" Georgie said, before picking up her champagne and taking a sip. "I shouldn't think you've got the energy for any of that after last weekend."

"Last weekend was a business trip." Brendon scowled.

"Hah, business, yes, if you're in the business." Georgie rolled her eyes. "Everyone knows that you and Timothy Hung-like-a-Donkey Curtis weren't interested in checking out that hotel in Brighton for a possible gig, you were just on a shagathon trip."

"Well, I take great offence to that, Georgie Porgy Pudding and Pie, because actually that's exactly what we did. Prada is looking at holding a launch party there for their new line of summer purses"

"Yes, we'll believe it when we see it." Georgie laughed and set down her glass.

Normally Megan's ears would have pricked at the mention of Prada summer purses — she loved purses for all seasons and all occasions — but not today.

"You want me to do that, Megan?"

"No, I can manage." The wrapper on the stocking box was proving tricky and her hands were a little shaky.

"Here." Georgie took the package and deftly opened it.

"Thanks." Megan smiled. She was so happy that her two best friends were with her today. She couldn't have done it without them. They were her rocks, her pillars of support, her port in a storm. They'd met over five years ago at a mutual friend's party, all newly single and all wanting to have some fun. Before long they'd been partying hard, but also kicking back and putting the world to rights together. Now they spoke or dropped in on each other most days, did lunch or met for cocktails every week, and tried to get away at least once each summer to worship the sun on some tropical beach.

"Don't look so worried," Georgie said with a slight frown.

"Yeah, are you okay?" Brendon asked.

"I'm fine, absolutely fine." Megan took a deep breath. "Come on, let's get this show on the road." She gathered the first stocking and carefully fed her right foot into it then pulled it up to her thigh. She repeated the action with her left and smoothed the lace holdup trims to ensure there were no creases.

"Ah, ah, one more thing before the dress." Georgie dipped into her handbag. "Here."

"A garter?" Megan queried. "Really? Isn't that kind of old-fashioned?"

"Of course it's old-fashioned, it's traditional." Brendon nodded seriously. "Something old, something new, something borrowed, something blue."

"Yes, you have to wear one. It would be bad luck otherwise." Georgie sank to her knees at Megan's feet, garter held into a wide 'O'. She smiled up at Megan. "The tiara is old, the dress is new and this is something borrowed and..." She twisted the garter to show off a tiny blue bow. "Is also blue."

"Oh, okay." Megan giggled at how serious her friends were taking this tradition. What was going to happen if she didn't have something old, new, borrowed and blue? It would hardly spoil the day or curse their marriage for all of time.

Would it?

Georgie slipped the garter up Megan's leg to her thigh.

Megan stroked her finger over the delicate white trim. It was very pretty and no doubt Dylan would enjoy removing it when they reached the bridal suite—possibly with his teeth.

"This dress is to die for," Brendon said, holding up Megan's voluminous gown. "All this taffeta, it's enough to sink a battleship."

"Yes, I'll certainly have to navigate carefully through doorways today," Megan said then took a sip of champagne. She set the glass aside. "Come on then, help me into the monster." She laughed.

Georgie didn't laugh with her, instead she sighed and clasped her hands under her chin.

"You okay, Georgie?" Megan asked.

"Yes, of course. I'm just so happy for you and that this day has finally come. We've all talked for years about who would be first to get hitched and now it's happening."

Megan reached for her hand and squeezed. "It will happen for you and Tom soon, I'm sure it will."

Georgie and Tom had been together for over a year and things were getting serious. They'd skied at Christmas, met the parents and both had a drawer at each other's apartment for spare clothes and toiletries – surely a sign of true commitment.

Megan shrugged. "Maybe, maybe not, but it doesn't matter today. Today is all about you and Dylan."

"Who is likely to be arriving at church with his best man as we speak," Brendon said, before clicking his tongue on the roof of his mouth. "There is an expectant groom waiting, so chop, chop ladies. Enough of this chatter, you two could talk for England."

"And you couldn't?" Georgie grinned.

It took both her friends to assist Megan into her dress. Luckily she could step into it, which meant her hair and makeup weren't in danger, but still, the sheer amount of material created quite a challenge.

Brendon fussed over the many hems, straightening the layers and fluffing it out so the periphery was even bigger. Georgie fiddled with the top, drawing up the side zipper and puffing the cupped silk sleeves.

"It's so beautiful," Georgie said wistfully.

"And so virginal," Brendon said, then cackled. "Except we know that's not true."

Megan skimmed her palms over the tight material at her waist then over her hips. Her hands became lost in the meringue nest of taffeta. "I've had some fun but I have standards." She rolled her eyes. "But not as much fun as you, Brendon."

"Yeah, well, I've not finished having fun yet," he said, standing. "There's many more fish out there for me to reel in and have my wicked way with."

"But don't you want to find the one?" Georgie asked, helping herself to a squirt of Megan's perfume.

"Yes of course, but not for a while. I've still got things I want to do, places to go, people to meet. I'm not ready to commit to one person, and besides, I wouldn't know if it was the right person anyway."

"What do you mean?" Megan asked, taking her perfume from Georgie and spritzing it over her neck and onto her wrists.

"Well, I don't know how you do it." He looked between them. "How you can be so sure you've met your soulmate? The man you're meant to be with for all of time. Go to bed with each night and wake up each morning next to."

"You'll just know," Georgie said.

"But how?" Brendon held up his palms. "How? Enlighten me."

"When you count the hours till you're going to see them again," Georgie said. "Think of them when planning what to eat that night so you know they'll enjoy it. Watch boring old war documentaries because that's their thing and not mind in the least because you're snuggled up on the sofa next to them. That's how you know."

Megan studied her friend. Georgie lit up when she talked of Tom. He'd captured her heart in a way no other man had. She'd never seen her so happy, so full of life—even the asthma that had always plagued her seemed to have settled. It was as if Tom's presence in her life was a soothing energy, a balm for her nerves. Megan hoped Tom would pop the question soon. It would feel so right to see Georgie in an elegant white gown walking down the aisle.

The door to the hotel room opened. Megan's mother, Iris, walked in carrying Gucci, who barked and wriggled as soon as he saw Brendon.

"Baby boy," Brendon said, rushing to pluck his tiny Pomeranian from Iris' arms. Gucci's little pink tongue rushed out to lick his master's chin and his tail waggled to a rapid tempo.

"Oh, Rose, my beautiful English Rose," Iris said, halting in her tracks as soon as she saw Megan. Her eyes misted and she pressed her lips together.

"Mum, you promised not to cry," Megan said, knowing that her mother would. She only ever called her Rose when she was feeling sentimental, and since she'd moved to Australia three years ago, she was more sentimental than ever when the family got together.

"I can't help it," Iris said. "My little girl all grown up and getting married."

"Yes, it seems that way." Megan smiled and fluffed the tulle on her dress. "What do you think?"

"I think you look beautiful. Dylan is lucky to have you. Very lucky indeed."

"Here, here to that." Georgie nodded.

"Abso-bloody-lutely," Brendon said, slipping a tiny doggie tuxedo over Gucci's head. It had a small bow tie beneath the chin, an embroidered waistcoat and tails that hung either side of Gucci's...tail.

Megan walked over to her mother and, stretching over the width of the dress, hugged her.

"No, no, please don't let me mess you up," Iris said, sniffing delicately.

"You won't mess me up, Mum, it's all fine." Megan placed a soft kiss on her mother's cheek. She smelt of lavender, as usual, and her skin was soft as satin.

"Oh, but I might." Iris gave Megan a frantic squeeze

then pulled away. "And you look so perfect. It all looks so perfect." She gestured at the door. "I've checked the cake and it's fabulous, exactly how Dylan wanted, a cascade of sparkling roses from the top tier to the base. The flowers are beautiful too, at the entrance to the reception room. The sweetest shade of baby pink and more gypsophila than you could shake a stick at."

"Good, that's good," Brendon said. "Flowers and cake are important."

"Where's Olivia?" Megan asked, wondering where her sister was. Olivia was her third bridesmaid.

"She's downstairs, with your father."

"I bet she looks beautiful." Megan adored how her bridesmaid dress complimented her sister's colouring. "What about Dad? Is he okay?" Megan asked, reaching for a tissue. She passed it to her mother, who instantly started checking her mascara hadn't run.

"He's fine with your sister, she's keeping an eye on him. She's good like that. You know, at calming him when he gets anxious."

"Yes, Olivia's great with him. But why's he anxious?" Megan hated seeing her father nervous. He was an all-round great guy, her rock, and as she'd grown from child to adult their relationship had only deepened. She loved him with all her heart.

"He's about to give away his eldest daughter, of course he's anxious. He's not so keen on giving away something so precious to him." Iris laughed but it held a note of tension. "And you most certainly are precious to him, Rose."

"Maybe he should look at it like he's gaining a son rather than giving away a daughter," Brendon said, ruffling Gucci's forehead so his fudge-coloured curls stood upright.

"I suppose," Iris said, sucking in a deep breath. "Yes, maybe that's how to look at it."

Megan studied her. She looked worried. Likely because Dad was stressed, even though he needn't be, he only had to walk a few steps down the aisle—not that she wouldn't be glad of his arm. Georgie was right, those heels, while stunning and one of her best designs yet, were hard to negotiate.

"Can you do me up?" Georgie asked, stepping in front of Megan. She'd pulled on her baby pink bridesmaid dress but the back zip was awkward for her to reach.

Megan slid it up. Georgie's hourglass frame suited the figure-hugging style perfectly and reminded her of a Marilyn Monroe photograph she'd seen once. Not least because Georgie's bubbles of blonde hair had just been cropped to jaw-length.

"Oh, Georgie," Iris said, "that dress is amazing on you. The colour is gorgeous with your skin tone and your eyes... simply stunning."

"Thank you," she said, turning back to Iris. "I'm glad Megan didn't pick lime green, I couldn't have pulled that off."

"I bet you could have worked lime green perfectly well." Megan laughed, though it was slightly forced because underneath Georgie's smile she knew there was a hint of longing. She wanted what Megan was about to have, a husband. But it would come soon, she was sure of it. Tom would eventually get around to it and bag the best thing that had ever happened to him.

"What about us?" Brendon said, striding in front of the mirror.

Gucci ran around his ankles, yapping as usual and hoping to be picked up again.

"How do we look?"

"Like the handsomest, gayest bridesmaid ever," Georgie said then laughed.

Megan reached to tickle Gucci beneath his chin but he wouldn't stay still for long enough, and besides, she could hardly reach him because of the dress. "And the handsomest doggie bridesmaid ever."

"Yes, I think we'll do." Brendon snapped down the pink satin waistcoat he wore beneath his morning suit. He then straightened the rose buttonhole. He looked good and he knew it. He even twirled around to check out his bum in the neat black trousers he wore, flicking up the tails of his morning coat to be sure.

"But we really should get going," Georgie said, again worrying about the time. "I know it's only a few minutes to the church from here but still, it's only ten minutes until the ceremony is due to start."

"Really?" Megan glanced at the clock that sat on the bedside table. Georgie was right. It was time to go.

It was time to go and get married.

And become Mrs Dunkin-Buckshaw.

Forever.

Her stomach clenched, the corset seeming to pull her muscles in even more.

Mr and Mrs Dylan Dunkin-Buckshaw.

The nerve endings in her scalp and at the base of her neck tingled. Maybe she should take Brendon's advice to her mother and look at it as not losing her name but gaining another family. There was Dylan's brother, his father and of course, his mother.

His mother. Rita. Who had been so excited about the wedding that Megan had actually stopped taking her calls in the final stages of preparation—not to be cruel, it was just too much. Her squeaky voice and over enthusiasm was draining, and Megan needed some energy left for the big day.

She'd called her yesterday, though, had bitten the bullet and picked up the phone. As she'd expected, it had been an hour of hysteria that had ranged from wild excitement to desperate despair because the napkins weren't the right shade of baby pink—how many shades of baby pink could there be?

"You okay, sweetpea?" Brendon took Megan's left hand.

"Yes, I think so." She looked at her hand in his. Her ring finger was bare, not even an indent. She'd hardly worn her engagement ring over the last six months, she'd been too worried about it getting wrecked at work with the glue she used on her designs. Now the ring was transferred to her right hand so that the new wedding band could be easily slipped on.

"You sure?" Georgie asked.

Megan pulled in as deep a breath as she could with the corset on. Her breasts pushed against the bones and she was aware of her heart thumping faster than normal.

"What is it?" Brendon asked.

"Nothing, nothing at all. I'm fine." Megan forced her mouth to turn up at the corners. "Really, let's get this show on the road."

"I'll see you there," her mother said. "Georgie and Brendon are very capable bridesmaids."

"And Gucci," Brendon added.

"And Gucci." Iris reached down and patted Gucci on the head. He licked her hand then ran excitedly in a circle.

"Yep, see you there, Mum," Megan said.

And next time we speak I'll be married.

"If I don't get the chance to say this to you later, Rose," her mother said, "know that I only ever want what is best for you. You make me so proud in everything you do, not least because you're a woman who knows what you want and you're not afraid to take it."

Megan felt her eyes tingle and her throat thicken. Tears were threatening.

A woman who knows what she wants and takes it.

More books from
Totally Bound Publishing

STACEY
SOLOMON

BEST THINGS IN LIFE

Walk on By

Parties...check
Gay best friend...check
Happiness...?

*Ever since Charlotte Taylor was a little girl she's wanted
fame and fortune.*

TOTALLY
BOUND

Never hump
an art thief.

Samantha Lytton
BOOK ONE

The Dimple
of Doom

LUCY WOODHULL

*Samantha Lytton is either going to end up in jail or
famous. Maybe both.*

About the Author

Jess Wright

Jessica Wright shot to fame in 2010 when she first appeared in the flagship ITV2 show The Only Way Is Essex. Jessica is one of the most loved and talked about stars in the UK. Jessica has proven her popularity with the nation by carving out a fashion career with her own e-commerce site and highly successful range at Lipstick Boutique. 2015 saw Jessica launching a career as a fiction author and releasing her first novel.

Jessica has 1.5 million followers on Twitter and 1.1 million followers on Instagram.

Jess Wright loves to hear from readers. You can find contact information, website details and an author profile page at https://www.totallybound.com/

Home of Erotic Romance

Printed in Great Britain
by Amazon